DAISIES FROM ASHES

SECOND EDITION

BY

SUMMER SELINE COYLE

ACACIA LEAF
PRESS

S S E Publishing & Acacia Leaf Press. Rothesay

DAISIES FROM ASHES SECOND EDITION

S S E Publishing & Acacia Leaf Press. Rothesay

ISBN 978-1-7781337-2-5

Technical Support and Formatting: Lyla Coyle

Set in the early seventies, DAISIES FROM ASHES delves into the lives of residents in a tenement building. The characters have formed a loyal, tight-knit family. They share dreams, celebrate one another's milestones, fall in love and plan their futures. Three strong, independent women, Joyce, Sandra, and Olivia have embarked on career changes in mid-life. As lives become altered in unimaginable ways, the three women rely on one another to deal with their catastrophic losses.

* * *

Sexual Content, Violence, Strong Language.

Jamie Ladd
5.0 out of 5 stars An engaging study of women's lives.
Reviewed in the United States on August 24, 2018
Amazon Verified Purchase
Exquisitely written, lovingly crafted.

The Selective Reader- Superbly written with compelling characters and an intricate plot.

This book was shortlisted for the 2021 Best Indie Book Award.

DAISIES FROM ASHES
SECOND EDITION

Table of Contents

Chapter 1/ The Sentinel
Chapter 2/ The Splendid
Chapter 3/ Early Spring
Chapter 4/ Bumper Cars
Chapter 5/ Little Girl Lost
Chapter 6/ Mustard And Teal
Chapter 7/ A Matter Of Honor
Chapter 8/ Family
Chapter 9/ Obstacle Course
Chapter 10/ Ravaged
Chapter 11/ Dark River
Chapter 12/ Hunters
Chapter 13/ Innocence
Chapter 14/ Last Days Of Summer
Chapter 15/ Insurance
Chapter 16/ Indian Summer
Chapter 17/ Relentless
Chapter 18/ The Offering
Chapter 19/ Tomorrows
Chapter 20/ Fragile
Chapter 21/ Greenfields
Chapter 22/ Beginnings

Chapter 23/ Shannon
Chapter 24/ Sacrifice
Chapter 25/ Love Is All
Chapter 26/ Don't Say Goodbye
Chapter 27/ Softly As I Leave You
Chapter 28/ The Bridge
Chapter 29/ Eternal Cycle
Chapter 30/ Daisies From Ashes

This novel is dedicated to my beautiful daughter, Lyla, who is a joy and an inspiration to me.

And:

In Memory of Sandra M.
Thank you, my dear friend, for your gift from the other side.

Chapter 1/ The Sentinel

I roam these streets late at night while the city sleeps. I am here when the rowdy bar patrons spill out to the sidewalks, indulging in regrettable pleasures. I am here long after taxicabs have transported them home and the stillness has returned. And, when the sun awakens, I am still here. I search relentlessly for tangible clues, and yet keep coming up empty.

An eerie silence looms over downtown Elmdale tonight. Yellow police tape and orange pylons encircle that lonely corner. I have waited six years for this day. Six agonizing years for an excavation to expose the carnage of that day. The boys at City Hall heard my silent pleas at last and chose to build the new bridge in this unlikely location.

* * *

Arlene was the first one to hear about it. She was pouring her first cup of coffee from the percolator into her pink ceramic mug with an enormous red "A" emblazoned on it.

"Arlene, dear, turn on the radio. The news is going to be on." her mother appeared in her burgundy velour robe.

Arlene switched on the turquoise Philco radio and sat across the ruby red chrome table from her mother. They listened solemnly in uncomfortable silence. Arlene rose swiftly and turned off the radio.

"You know something, don't you?" her mother raised one eyebrow.

"It's too early to speculate, Mama. I have to get a move on."

"This early?" her mother shoved a forkful of scrambled eggs into her mouth, "Aren't you going to have your breakfast, dear?"

"I lost my appetite."

"Then, I'll help myself to it. No use letting perfectly good food go to waste."

"Sure, go ahead." Arlene ran up the stairs.

Her mother sighed. The yellow Priscilla curtains above the sink were coated with grease stains. The cabinet doors were in dire need of a fresh coat of white paint.

"I'm off now, Mama." Arlene returned with her pocketbook and kissed her on the cheek.

"Arlene, what do you think about new curtains for the kitchen? Maybe a whole new color scheme?"

"Why don't we talk about it tonight?"

"You don't have to rush off this early, dear. You're your own boss now."

"I thought I'd get an early start and get the shop all spic and span."

"Can you pick up some pork chops from Valor Meat Market on your way home, dear?"

"Sure, Mom. Bye!" Arlene flew past her.

"Bye, dear." her mother called out, but she only heard the front door slamming shut.

* * *

Olivia was the second one to hear about it on the eight o'clock news. Her schedule was flexible that morning, and she had awakened from an additional hour of sleep. Enjoying her luxurious coffee from her Mr. Coffee machine, she was lounging in her purple silk pajamas, stretched out on her mint green sectional, paying little attention to the radio until the news came on. Her mug came crashing down on the wood floor, a pool of dark liquid spreading unnoticed. She screamed until her throat hurt.

She frantically dialled her telephone.

"Janet, can you please cancel my appointments for the day?" she said hoarsely, "Something's come up and I need to be somewhere else."

"Certainly, Dr. Cordova."

"Thank you, Janet."

Her knees raised to her chin, Olivia sat curled up in a corner, sobbing uncontrollably.

* * *

Joyce was the third one to hear about it on the nine o'clock news. Dressed in her brown tweed suit, she was about to turn off her radio when the news came on.

She reached for her rotary dial telephone and dialled the numbers with a pencil.

"Josie, I'm cancelling all of my classes for today."

"Yes, Ma'am."

"Thank you, dear."

Joyce dialled the phone again and waited for it to ring nine times before it was picked up and a faint voice was on the other end.

"Liv, are you all right, sweetheart?"

She heard muffled sobs.

"I'll be right over."

* * *

Sandi was the last one to learn about it. She was in a coffee shop on King Street, fortifying her diminutive frame with black coffee and a raspberry Danish as she reviewed briefs before court.

"Sandi! I'm so glad I found you!" a young woman in office attire burst in and sat across the table.

"What's up, Ruthie?"

"I heard something gruesome on the radio and I immediately thought of you."

"I'm not sure I like the sound of that." Sandi winked.

“Didn’t you use to live in a building on the corner of Queen and Westmorland when you were in law school?”

“I did. What did you hear?”

“When they were doing all that excavation for the new bridge, the workers ran into some trouble.”

“Trouble?”

“Dead people.”

“Ruthie, this is one heck of a way to start the day.” Sandi gathered her papers and placed them back in her briefcase, “I’m due in court in a little while. I’ll see you back at the office after I’m done.”

“Do you know who they are?”

“We need to sit tight and be patient until they have more information.”

“This is really creeping me out.”

“I promise you, everything is going to turn out all right, Ruthie.” Sandi patted her on the shoulder, “I’ll see to it that it does.”

* * *

The veil of the morning mist has lifted to welcome a sunny spring day. I can no longer feel the warmth of the sun on my skin or the chill of the rain in my bones. I died six years ago. I cannot cross over to be with my Harold until the truth has been revealed and justice has been served. This is where I am needed for now.

Chapter 2/ The Splendid

Splendid Hotel was our home, our refuge from a world that was all too rapidly changing around us. We were ordinary people with ordinary lives. None of us had much, but in those days, there was not as much to be had. It was easy to be content. A radio, a phonograph, a dozen or so 45 rpm records, one or two Long Play records, a small television in a corner perched on a flimsy metal stand, a warped bookcase with a few classics, a library card, restaurants and movie theaters nearby. None of us needed more. Most of us did not even own cars. There was not a corner of Elmdale we could not reach on foot. We each had our dreams, hopes, and fantasies. For some, those fantasies were to explode into reality and devour them.

Harold and I moved into "The Splendid" in 1957. I was the office manager at the optometrist's office five doors up the street. Harold sold shoes at Zeeman's Department Store. Myrtle was living there even back then, humming to herself as she went up and down the stairs, the pungent odor of her cigarettes announcing her presence. You could hear her cursing when things did not go her way. George and Ethel had the same front apartment and he was our superintendent even then. The tenants were young secretaries and shop clerks, retired widows, and older gentlemen who stared blankly at the street all day from their windows. The young folks did not stay long. The Splendid was a temporary sojourn on the way to a more desirable destination. The long-term tenants eventually ended up in nursing homes or departed this world. Seasons melted into one another year after year.

In 1967, I lost my Harold. I vowed I would never leave our apartment. I felt his presence with me there. In 1968, the building was bought by a police officer, Frank Elliott, or "Sarge", as we all called him. He ran a tight ship and rented only to quiet, respectable tenants. His son Mel, who was also on the police force, and the first member of our chosen family, took an apartment on my floor. Fresh-faced, unassuming Nadya, the second member of our family, burst on the scene in 1970. Soon, our little doll, Arlene moved in. Greg, Mel's friend and colleague was next. Then, it was Olivia, a striking, doe-eyed graduate student. Gayle was the one to cause a stir with her arrival. Elmdale harbored shameful secrets of racist undercurrents at the time. It was not until after the flood of 1973 that Joyce, another graduate student, arrived, soon followed by Sandra, the no-nonsense law student in June. Steve arrived shortly after that. July gifted us with our dear Vincent.

* * *

With her rhinestone-studded cat glasses and her moss green Spanish scarf covering her head full of metal curlers, Myrtle came up the stairs, a cigarette hanging out of the corner of her mouth painted the color of raw liver.

"Those are bad for you, Myrtle." Mel remarked jovially.

"You mind your own beeswax, you little whipper-snapper." she shot back.

"Just looking out for your health, Myrtle."

"Never you mind, young man. You worry about your own health."

"I do. I take good care of myself."

"Hmph." she scowled, "You're gonna get venereal disease, the way you go around with them colored girls."

"You have a lovely day, too, Myrtle." he shook his head.

In the lobby, he noticed the mortified expression on Nadya's face.

"This town is full of bigots and rednecks like Myrtle." he told her, "I could tell you stories that would make your hair stand on end. Most landlords still refuse to rent to black tenants."

"How can people be like that?"

"I don't know, Nadya. I wish there could be more gentle folks like you. The world would be a better place. Take care. Peace, sister."

"Peace, Mel."

"You ought to hear what she says about you." Ethel, who had been listening from her apartment, waited for Mel to leave, and opened her door, "She calls you "The Communist Girl"."

Nadya was only too aware that Ethel appeared to relish informing her of this tidbit.

"She ain't too fussy about the Eye-talian girl, either. Calls 'er "The Mafia Princess"."

Nadia shook her head and walked away.

Ethel's next stop on her mission was my apartment. There was no use pretending I was not home.

"Blanchie, I swear, this town is going to hell in a hand basket!" she flopped herself down on my gold brocade sofa, "Got any sherry?"

"It's too early in the day, Ethel. I can make some tea."

"Got anything stronger. Any Nescafe?"

"Sure, I can make you some Nescafe." I filled my avocado green whistling kettle and placed it on my front electric burner, "I only keep it around for when you drop in, anyway, Ethel. I don't care for the stuff myself."

"You're too finicky, Blanche."

"I have my indulgences."

"Sure you do. Pasta doesn't count."

"It does, when Mama Rosa makes it."

Ethel droned on but I found it difficult to focus my attention on her.

"You know, she wouldn't be bad looking if she wore some make-up, fixed her hair, and wore decent clothes. She looks like a pauper."

"Who?" I returned to the room with her instant coffee, "Mama Rosa?"

"Your young friend, the bookkeeper. She makes no effort to look attractive to men."

"Nadya is a very pretty girl. She doesn't need to tart herself up to impress men."

"There are so many young people living here now, it makes me nervous."

"Why?"

"They play hippie music, sit on the fire escape...This place just ain't the way it used to be."

"The tenants, for the most part are mature, responsible adults, holding down jobs, and working toward post-graduate degrees. There are a few younger students but they don't cause any trouble. Who cares if they try to unwind with some music?"

"There are strange things going on, Blanchie. I see these cars slowing down and the drivers looking up at the windows all the time. It's giving me the heebie-jeebies."

"They might be undercover cops looking for drug dealers."

"Drug dealers? Here?"

"I'm funning you, Ethel. You've been watching too many stories on T.V. You think there are crooks hiding around every corner."

"George says there's a rich businessman named Bok Heller buying all the buildings around here. He's already bought most of the places across the street, nearly to the corner of York."

"I don't believe Mr. Silver would ever sell, Ethel. His family's owned that department store since '54."

"This fellow's bought everything else around "Silver's". He's been hounding Sarge to sell "The Splendid", too. George says Sarge flat out refused him."

"I wonder what this fellow wants with all these old places. He's most likely planning to tear them all down, build new, shiny places so he can charge exorbitant rents."

"It don't matter now 'cause Sarge ain't selling." Ethel crossed the room to my television set and switched it on. She turned the dial to the channel she wanted and returned to her seat.

I left Ethel to indulge in her daily game show fix and peered out at the weary rag-tag assortment of storefronts - most of them turn of the century or post World War One ornate red brick, with more austere mid-century structures elbowing their way in, demanding recognition. What would a businessman want with crumbling buildings housing modest small businesses and a tenement of undetermined vintage with an obscure history?

Chapter 3/ Early Spring

"Put those eyes back in your head, son." Mel said.

Greg's enormous dark eyes were transfixed on the woman at a nearby table, drinking coffee and writing in a notebook.

"She's definitely captured your attention." Gayle remarked.

"I can't believe I never really noticed her before."

"Believe me, she's not your type." Mel said, "Too wholesome."

"There's something about her. An air of mystery." Greg murmured.

"Forget it, pal. You won't even get to first base with her for months."

"There's more to a relationship than sex."

Mel felt Greg's forehead with his palm.

"Relationship!" Gayle laughed, "You must be delirious with the swine flu, Mr. Love'm and Leave'm."

"I don't think she's ready for the likes of you, Greg Logan." Mel said.

"What is that supposed to mean?" he shot back.

"You don't have the best track record for monogamy, I'm afraid, Greg." Gayle said apologetically.

"Unlike Mr. Holier-Than-Thou here."

"Don't get hot under the collar, buddy. Just joshing. If you want to ask her out, go for it."

"I don't want to scare her." Greg frowned, "She looks so fragile, so innocent..."

"I think the two of you would make a very cute couple, Greg." Gayle said, "She wouldn't be scared. I think she would be flattered. Have you looked in the mirror lately?"

"Thanks for your vote of confidence, Gayle."

"She's a sweet, gentle soul, and she could get terribly hurt if she gets involved with someone who doesn't appreciate her or treat her right. Just be careful with her heart, Greg. Be sensitive when you want to break it off somewhere down the road."

"Who says I'd ever want to break it off with her, if I were lucky enough to have her?"

"The boy's smitten." Mel winked at Gayle, "You've been checking her out pretty closely for weeks now. You haven't even looked at another woman. What happened to the hot mama you took to the Valentine party at City Lights Lounge?"

"You mean Cheri? She's too high on herself. It was doing my head in."

"How about another round of java to keep us awake at work tonight?" Mel motioned to their waiter.

Families with young children were arriving. Laughter and giggles filled the restaurant.

"Daddy, look, cops!" a young boy pointed in their direction, noticing their uniforms.

The chestnut-haired woman turned around to smile at the child and met Greg's gaze. Both of them smiled shyly. She gathered her belongings and stood up to put on her coat. Greg's eyes followed her as she approached the young man at the cash register to pay for her coffee. On her way out of the restaurant through the door leading to the apartment lobby, she cast one final glance in his direction. As their eyes locked, he became aware of her quivering lower lip.

"Earth to Greg." Mel punched his arm playfully.

Greg did not notice.

* * *

She took a seat at a table by the window and removed her pale blue trench coat. Folding it meticulously, she placed it on one of the empty chairs. Mama Rosa approached her and pinched her cheek.

"How are you doing today, my darling?"

"Just fine, Mama Rosa." she smiled, "How is your day?"

"Can't complain, dear. Can't complain. Your smile lights up this whole place."

"That's so kind of you to say, Mama Rosa."

"You coffee's coming along shortly. It's already paid for."

She furrowed her brow in bewilderment.

"The nice young officer at that table." she gestured in the direction of a small table where Greg was seated, "I'll be back with your coffee."

Greg waved tentatively and smiled nervously. She smiled and motioned him to join her. He complied sheepishly and sat beside her.

"Hi." he said.

"Thank you."

"Don't mention it. I've noticed you appreciate a strong cup of Joe as much as I do."

"You drink yours black, too." she glanced at his cup.

"It's the only way."

"Here you are, dear." Mama Rosa returned with her coffee, "Enjoy your coffee and each other's company." she winked at them.

"She's so nice." she said.

"She's a terrific lady. I'm Greg, by the way." he extended his hand awkwardly.

"I'm Nadya." she shook his hand.

"I know."

"I know who you are, too." she scrunched up her nose.

"I live in #4."

"I'm in #8."

"I knew that, too."

"So did I."

Both burst into laughter.

"Your last name's Logan."

"I know yours, too, but there's no way I can pronounce it."

"Don't worry. Nobody can."

"Why don't you teach me? I want to be the only person who can pronounce it."

"It's Babayevski." she enunciated slowly.

"Babayevski." he repeated, "How did I do?"

"Perfect."

"I feel very smart now."

She laughed softly.

"Logan's an Irish name, isn't it?" she asked tentatively.

"Sure is."

"You look Irish."

"Is that good or bad?"

"It's good. Very good." she blushed.

"Thank you. I'm afraid I don't know if you look Slavic, because I've never met a Slavic lady before."

She laughed, a less self-conscious laugh this time.

"You work at Newman and Carr Office Supplies, don't you? Do you like it there?"

"Very much. I work mainly in the back office. All my co-workers are older ladies, so it's a very pleasant environment. What you do, Greg, is the most honorable, most altruistic profession. You risk your life everyday to keep the rest of us safe."

"That's very kind of you. Thank you. I appreciate that."

Mama Rosa arrived to ask if they wanted more coffee. Both of them smiled and nodded.

"Nadya," he said, "I hope this isn't intrusive: I've noticed you writing in a notebook."

"It's not intrusive at all. I write poetry and short stories. It makes me happy. I don't know if it's any good, but I feel a compulsion to keep doing it."

"That's an amazing talent. I don't have a creative bone in my body. I just play basketball with a bunch of guys a couple of times a week. That's what I do to make myself happy."

"We all need to do what works for us."

"I agree."

"It seems a lot of people set the bar so high for what they need in order to be happy, that they spend their entire lives chasing elusive dreams, not experiencing happiness. Even if a person doesn't have the things they long for most, they can find happiness in the small things, the things that provide an escape from the reality of what's lacking."

"Wow! That's profound." his eyes widened.

"Thank you. I haven't thought of it as being profound before. It's just an outlook that helps me survive."

"You're amazing. I've got to give this some serious thought now. People always talk about material things or selfish pleasures: They want to see the world, stay in luxurious hotels, buy expensive cars, houses, boats. They want private schools for their kids, and everything else money can buy. When they get all they strive for, it's not enough. There's always another elusive goal. They're never happy."

"The less we want, the more happiness we experience...A sunny day, a beautiful song, time spent with a beautiful soul, a good book..."

"Having this talk with you makes me happy."

"Thank you. Me, too." she blushed.

"I hope we can have more talks like this."

"I'd like that."

"Tell you what: When I'm working nights like today, I'll wait here for you to come back from work."

"That's very nice of you, Greg."

"My pleasure. I can't think of any conversation I enjoyed this much."

"Me, too."

"When I'm working days, I have the entire evening free...Can we..."

"I would like that." she smiled reassuringly.

"I'm working nights all this week. See you tomorrow at the same time, then?"

"I'll be here."

"I'll have to get to work now. I'll look forward to seeing you tomorrow. Have a good night, Nadya."

"You, too, Greg. Please be safe out there."

He rose awkwardly and shook her hand. As he walked across the restaurant, he paused in the doorway, turned around and waved. She waved back with a smile.

* * *

"How's Nadya?" Mel winked as he emptied his mailbox.

"She's fine." Greg cast him a suspicious glance.

"You've been living like a monk since you met her. When are you going to get her in the sack?"

"Don't talk about her like that!" Greg snapped, "She's not that kind of girl."

"Ooh. Touched a nerve there." Mel smirked, "You've got it bad for her, don't you?"

"Cut it out, Mel. She's not like other women. We're taking things slow. I don't want to pressure her into anything she's not ready for."

"How will you know when she's ready? She's not the type to let you know. She's waiting for you to take the initiative. At this rate, you're never going to get it on, both of you waiting for the other to make a move."

"We'll work it out somehow."

* * *

Greg was waiting for her at Mama Rosa's with two coffees to go in Styrofoam cups with plastic lids.

"Do you want to have these up on the fire escape?" he suggested, "It's 65 degrees out. I thought we'd get some fresh air."

"Sounds good to me."

The wooden fire escapes were accessed through heavy doors at the far end of the hallways on the second and third floors. The white paint was a murky grey-brown, peeling to expose the aged wood underneath.

“You’ve got furniture out here.” she observed the folding lawn chairs, the cable spool table, the royal blue plastic milk crates and the portable turntable balanced on top of them.

“I was hoping you’d agree to come up here, so I got these out of the storage room in the basement – except for the record player. That one’s mine.”

“Greg, this is so nice.” she took her coffee from him and placed it on the rough wood cable spool.

“Are you cold?” he placed his own cup on the floor, “I can get you a sweater.”

“No – no. I’m fine.”

“There’s quite a wind coming from the river. I don’t want you to catch a cold.”

“I’m all right – really. Thank you.”

“If you get cold, let me know.”

“I will.”

“Have a seat, Nadya. If you’ll excuse me for a moment, there’s something I have to get.” he opened his bedroom window from the outside and climbed in.

She took the chair beside the makeshift table. He returned with two paper plates and a small cardboard box.

“I hope you like eclairs.”

“I love them. Greg, you went to so much trouble.”

“No trouble at all. I got these at the bakery across the street.” he gave her a plate, opened the box and held it before her, “This time, we don’t need to rush off. We both have the rest of the day off.”

“This is so nice.” she took one éclair and placed it on her plate.

“Are the eclairs okay?”

She took a dainty bite and nodded, wiping custard crème from her lips with a fingertip.

“They’re delicious. So fresh.”

“We can make this our ritual. We can have coffee and eclairs up here. It’s almost spring.” he took an éclair for himself and bit into it.

"I would like that."

"Do you have plans for the weekend, Nadya?"

"No."

"Would you like to see a movie?"

"I would love to."

"Maybe we could have a bite first..."

"That would be nice."

She studied his profile. Men like Greg did not pay attention to wallflowers like her. Moments like this were beyond her comprehension. Catching her eyes on his face, he laughed.

"Do I have food on my face? Do I look stupid?"

"No, no, no." she protested, "I'm sorry. I made you uncomfortable."

"You didn't. But I am getting you that sweater." he returned to his room via his preferred route and returned with a hunter green cable-knit pullover. It must bring out his beautiful green eyes, she mused, easing into it and smoothing it over her hips.

"Why don't we listen to music?" he suggested, "I hope you like Percy Faith. I borrowed the record from a guy at work. He recommended it, but I wasn't sure you'd like it."

"Easy listening is my kind of music."

"That's a relief. I'll get it now and play it for us." he climbed in his window again and returned with a Long Play album. He left his window open a crack and fed the record player cord through it. He climbed back in to plug it into the nearest receptacle in his room. He placed the record on the turntable and lowered the needle. Soft music filled the air.

"You've gone to so much trouble."

"No trouble. It's fun." he resumed his seat, "Have more eclairs. But remember, we're having dinner at Mama Rosa's later, so save some room."

"You're so nice to me, Greg."

"Nice to you? Nadya, you deserve to be treated like royalty."

"Thank you." she bit her lower lip, blinking away her tears.

His hand instinctively reached for hers.

“Let’s dance.” he suggested; rising from his chair, he took both of her hands and lifted her to her feet.

A thousand volts of electricity shot through her spine. Afraid her eyes might betray her, she buried her face in his chest, quivering under his touch. He smelled like Irish Spring soap. His heart was beating as fast as hers. When he released her, she kept her eyes lowered. He took her hands and raised them to his lips. And, at that moment, for the first time in her life, she felt beautiful, desirable, clever, and deserving of all good things.

Chapter 4/ Bumper Cars

"Ethel and Arlene are still noticing cars slowing down in front of the building." Gayle locked her mailbox, "Arlene's feeling nervous about living in a front apartment. She thinks they might be Peeping Toms."

"They are here for a specific reason, looking for a specific person." Mel said.

"Could be loan sharks looking for a guy who doesn't pay his gambling debts." Gayle said.

"One of the cars Arlene keeps seeing has a well-dressed woman driving it." Greg said, "She got the licence number and I checked her out. She's a civil servant. These people can't be looking for anyone at The Splendid. We don't have any gamblers, winos, or other shady characters here and it makes no sense for a government employee to be involved in an illegal plot."

"Wait!" Gayle said, "Didn't George say some big shot wanted to buy this place?"

"Dad told him on no uncertain terms that he would not sell." Mel said.

"Maybe he's trying some not-so-friendly persuasion." Greg remarked.

"If Arlene can get more licence numbers, we'll be able to get some answers soon." Mel said.

"Sh-h. Someone's coming down the stairs." Gayle whispered.

As Nadya appeared on the landing, Greg beamed.

"Hi, honey." he approached her and kissed her cheek.

"Hi, Greg." she kissed him back on his cheek.

"Where are you off to?" he asked her.

"Only to "Eat Rite" for a few groceries."

"Mind if I tag along?"

"I'd like that." she smiled at Gayle and Mel, "I didn't mean to interrupt your conversation."

"You didn't." Gayle reassured her, "You two have fun. See you later."

"Bye." she took the arm Greg offered.

Neither one of them noticed the rusty Comet speeding behind them until it swung on to the sidewalk and came within inches of them. Greg instinctively enclosed her in his arms and pulled her away swiftly.

"I've got you." he led her to the bench outside Eat Rite, "I've got his licence number. I'm going to nail him."

While keeping one arm around her, he reached in his pocket and produced a notepad and a pen. He uncapped the Bic pen with his teeth and wrote down the licence number.

"Who is this guy? Why is he trying to run you down, Nadya?"

"I've never seen him before."

"I ran the licence number Arlene gave me a couple of days ago. It's a woman named Hortense Desmond. She's an accountant at the Department of Agriculture."

"That's where my dad works."

"The plot thickens. I saw her tailing you on your way home from work yesterday. When you came into the restaurant to meet me, she stopped right outside the window and looked in directly at us. She stayed there for quite a while, too. I took down her licence number and it was the same one. Is this chick your dad's girlfriend or something?"

"I don't think so."

"Maybe she's a jealous wife or girlfriend of a guy you were involved with."

"I haven't been involved with anyone in over ten years – and even then, it wasn't really what you could call an involvement."

"What does this woman want with you? And who is this guy tonight?"

"I don't understand any of this, Greg."

"You're shivering." he pulled her close, "I'm not going to let anyone hurt you, Nadya. I won't let you out of my sight, even if it means camping out on your sofa."

"Thank you." she murmured softly.

"I'm going to catch these lowlifes and when I do, they're going to wish they'd never been born."

"I remember something that happened last week – but I don't know if it has any connection to this."

"What happened?"

"I was in the lobby, collecting my mail from my mailbox. These two men came in and looked around. I've never seen them before. I kept my head down, locked up and ran up the stairs as fast as I could."

"Did you get a look at them? Can you describe them?"

"Not too well. One was middle aged...thin...short grey hair, glasses, well-dressed...Very ordinary looking. The other one was younger, had long hair, kind of a greasy brown, and he was dressed in jeans and a jean jacket."

"You described them very well. I'm going to do whatever it takes to get these scumbags...Nadya, honey, why don't we forget the groceries for tonight? Are you okay for a while?"

She nodded.

"Let's go to Mama Rosa's." he helped her up and wound an arm around her shoulder.

She placed her own arm around his waist. At Mama Rosa's, they were ushered to a table by the window.

"You might need something stronger than coffee after what just happened." he reached across the table and squeezed her hands.

"I think you're right."

When the waiter came to the table, she ordered vodka on the rocks.

"I'll have the same." he said, "You're full of surprises." he told her, once the waiter was gone.

She blushed.

“You’re this lovely fragile flower. You live a clean, modest life. You’ve undoubtedly gone through things most people could not even fathom, and you’ve emerged beautifully. Then, you have people following you, trying to run you down, and you don’t know who or why. Then you drink straight vodka.”

“I wish we could all leave our past in the past and live our lives as the new people we’ve evolved into.” she said.

“Sounds good to me. I wouldn’t mind leaving my past behind.”

“It has a way of coming back to haunt us at every turn.”

“It’s going to be all right, Nadya.” he squeezed her hand.

The waiter served their drinks.

“I’m not proud of some of the things I’ve done in the past.” she drank half of her drink at once, “I did stupid, desperate things, ended up making enemies, because I was in so much pain. I just wanted the pain to go away.”

“They can’t hurt you anymore.” he murmured, “I’m here.”

“It’s so wrong to judge people by their past. If someone genuinely wants to change and grow, they can transcend their old selves. Of course, some people never regret their past transgressions, so they never change.”

“You never cease to amaze me, my beautiful lady.”

“I must be boring you.” she blushed.

“On the contrary, this is the least bored I’ve ever been in my life.”

“You’re the most amazing man I’ve ever met, Greg.”

“I’m not sure I deserve that, but I’ll take a compliment any way I can get it.”

“You’re a Scorpio, aren’t you?” she smiled playfully.

“How did you know that?” his eyes widened.

“I just know.”

“Is it good or bad?”

“The very best.”

“Why, thank you, Ma’am.” he flashed his impish grin, “I’m afraid there’s no way I can guess your sign.”

"Cancer."

"Then, Cancer is the very best zodiac sign."

He ordered more drinks. Neither one noticed Gayle and Mel entering the restaurant from the apartment lobby and approaching their table.

"Fancy meeting the two of you here." Gayle said.

"Hi, Mommy and Daddy." Greg arched his eyebrows.

"You need to watch out for this one, Nadya." Mel said, "He's pretty slippery."

"He'll ply you with booze to get you in the sack." Gayle winked at her.

"Greg's always a perfect gentleman." Nadya said.

"Have fun, guys." Gayle patted her on the shoulder.

"Don't do anything I wouldn't do." Mel winked at Greg and followed Gayle to their table.

"I don't think anyone could get you drunk and take advantage of you. Not that I'd ever think about doing that to you."

"It never crossed my mind, even at the beginning before I got to know you."

"I think it's despicable to do that to a woman." he frowned, "You're not even tipsy. I'll bet you could drink anyone under the table any day."

From their nearby table, their friends observed them fondly.

* * *

She opened the door to find Greg in his uniform.

"Am I under arrest, Officer?" she asked playfully.

"Don't give me any ideas. I won't be able to concentrate on anything at work tonight." he carried a brown paper bag into her kitchen, "These are some groceries I thought you could use. I tried to guess what you'd like."

"Greg, I can't believe you'd do this for me." tears filled her eyes, "Now I know why you brought me upstairs early. I thought you'd been called to go to work earlier."

"I didn't want you to waste away from starvation."

"How much do I owe you?" she went into the bedroom for her purse.

"You don't owe me anything."

"Please let me pay."

"I won't hear of it."

"Then, let me cook dinner for you this weekend. Is that okay?"

"That would be terrific."

"You're so wonderful." she flung her arms around him.

Caught unaware, he leaned in to kiss her. The passionate response he received came as much of a surprise to her as it did him. He kissed her long and hard. Every fiber of her being was longing to surrender in wild abandon.

"Do you have any idea what you're doing to me?" he whispered in her ear, "Why don't I come back here tomorrow after you get off work, so we can resume this? I have the next three days off."

She pulled him back for another long kiss.

"If I don't go now, I'll never get to work." he said, "I'm going to be thinking about tomorrow the whole time."

"Are you going to cuff me?"

"You'll just have to wait and see, my lovely. We'll go out to dinner first."

"I'll be thinking about you the whole time, too." she was her shy self again.

"Lock this door after me and don't open it for anybody, okay?" he kissed her softly.

"I promise." she caressed his dimpled cheek, "Stay safe."

Chapter 5/ Little Girl Lost

Completing any task at work was a challenge. Her concentration shot to pieces, she found herself re-doing every task multiple times. This did not escape the eyes of her supervisor.

"Honey, you look green around the gills." Margaret patted her on the back.

"I'm feeling under the weather, Marg."

"Take the rest of the day off and get some rest. By Monday, you'll be good as new."

The excursion to the drug store was excruciating. Keeping her head down, praying no one would recognize her, she selected the only option for an impromptu situation. Relatively unreliable, however uncomplicated, it would have to do. She avoided eye contact with the self-assured, pretty clerk who rang in her purchase and once outside, attempted to conceal the semi-opaque paper bag.

She was worldly enough to be aware what his expectations were, but not worldly enough to satisfy them. How long would it take for him to walk away? There was no question that he would; it was only a question of when.

She did not own expensive, high quality lingerie or a proper dress for a date, and could not afford to acquire any of those on short notice. She would not even know where to look or what to look for. Hopefully, he wouldn't notice.

Slinking into her apartment unnoticed by anyone in the building, she concealed her purchase in the cabinet under the bathroom sink. She showered with meticulous care and dressed in the only dress she considered passable: A pale blue floral one with a flared skirt and a sash that tied in the back. It had never been worn, but bought with the far-fetched fantasy of a date in mind, though it was far less attractive than the dresses other women wore. And, here she was, wearing it for a date. A date. What a foreign concept it was to her. The few men who had plodded through her life had attached a completely different meaning to the word.

She applied her make-up diligently, choosing a pale blue eye shadow and a soft pink lipstick as her only cosmetics. She splashed on "Khadine" cologne. Brushing her chestnut wavy hair, she pinned a white silk flower to one side. Her heart was playing a deafening drum beat in trepidation. Her lack of experience was bound to turn him off. If she disappointed him, and drove him away, it would become awkward to be running into each other in the building. Would he let her down gently the way fictional heroes did, and treat her in a civilized manner after ending it with her, or would he behave like real-life men and pepper her generously with put-downs and jeer at her when their paths crossed?

She put on a record to calm her nerves as she waited. Ella Fitzgerald was singing "Reaching For The Moon" when she heard the soft knock on the door.

He was dressed in a stone-white summer suit, holding a bouquet of delicate flowers, his deep dimples sheltering an earnest smile. No one had ever given her flowers. Heck, no one had even put the time and effort into picking dandelions off the side of the road as an offering.

"Hi." she smiled weakly.

"Hi yourself. Look at you."

"Is this okay?"

"You're gorgeous!" he kissed her cheek and handed her the bouquet.

"Thank you." she blushed, "You look very handsome."

"Thank you."

"I'll put these in water. They're so beautiful." she lowered her eyes.

He followed her to the kitchen and wrapped his arms around her from behind. As she filled a glass vase from the cupboard with water and arranged the Marguerite daisies, pink carnations, and baby's breath with care, he kissed her neck.

What she was feeling for him was so frighteningly intense that, she believed she might lose her mind completely or die right there.

He pinned her against the wall and kissed her in a way no one else ever had. She fumbled with his tie and shirt buttons. He tossed his jacket across the living room. His tie took flight from her hands and she kissed his bare chest feverishly, attempting to remove his open shirt. Under his skillful fingers, her dress and undergarments fell to the floor with the fluidity of petals from a dying flower. She leapt into his arms, and with her legs wound around him, he carried her into the bedroom. A bolt of lightning shot through her the moment he entered her. In the hot summer air, her primal screams of ecstasy overpowered all other sounds in the building. Neither one of them heard Myrtle banging on her ceiling with a broom handle. When they collapsed in each other's arms, she was overcome with uncontrollable tremors. He held her tenderly until it subsided. By now, Myrtle was shouting profanities at them.

"That just blew my mind." he kissed her hair, "You're incredible."

"It was you."

"It was the two of us together." he kissed her hand.

* * *

"We never did get to have that dinner." he said, "I'm going to make it up to you."

"You don't have to worry about that, Greg. I can whip something up for us. What would you like?"

"You...Only you." he caressed her cheek, "It's dark out. We didn't come up for air all this time, but I don't want to come up for air yet."

"Neither do I."

A loud banging was heard at the door.

"Open up! I know youse two are in there!"

"It's Myrtle." he raised his expressive eyebrows, "Do you want me to take care of her? Otherwise, she won't go away."

Her pink floral bedspread wrapped around him, he skipped over their scattered clothes to open the door.

"Youse should be ashamed of yourselves!" Myrtle shook her index finger at him, "Disgraceful heathens! Carryin' on like alley cats over my head! I'm going to tell Sarge about this. He's going to throw you out on your ears. Youse two are going to rot in hell."

"I'm sorry we disturbed you, Myrtle. We'll try to keep it down."

"Make sure you do."

"I promise. Scout's honor."

"Look at the state of you...The state of this place...Disgraceful." she shook her head and turned to leave.

He shut the door behind her and returned to Nadya's waiting arms.

* * *

There was a loud knock at the door.

"Let's ignore it." he mumbled, his face buried in her breasts.

"What if it's important?"

"Unless the building's on fire, it's not important."

"Nadya, open this door now!" a female voice called out in Azerbaijani as the knocking became louder.

"Somebody's in a foul mood out there." he said.

"It's my mother."

"She has great timing." he stifled his laughter.

"Nadya, open this door this minute, or I swear I'll get the superintendent to open it!"

"Okay, this time, I heard the word superintendent in plain English, and I know where this is headed." he scrambled to his feet.

She wrapped her long blue robe around her and motioned to him to stay in the bedroom, closing the door behind her. She gathered their clothes off the floor and wrapped them in the green afghan from the sofa. She tucked the bundle into the linen closet.

"What took you so long?" the older woman in the linen suit demanded.

"I dozed off. I'm taking cold medicine."

"Something's not right here." the woman sniffed, "I can smell it. You've got a man here."

"No."

"I smell a man."

"There was a plumber here earlier fixing the sink."

"No. I smell a naked man. You've got a man hiding somewhere." she barged into the bedroom to find an empty but rumpled bed, "Where is he?"

"There's no one here."

"Don't lie to me!" she slapped her face, "You smell like you've just had sex. You filthy, cheap, ugly whore!"

"Come on, Ana, let's go." the dark-haired man in the business suit took her arm.

"Aren't you as disgusted as I am, Boris?"

"We can discuss it at home."

"No, I want to discuss it here and now! What are we going to do about the way our daughter has turned out?"

"It was obvious a long time ago that she had loose morals. We've tried everything to control her, but she's beyond hope. Let's go home, Ana. This is a lost cause. I don't want any more to do with her. She's no longer my daughter."

"What are the neighbors going to think? They must be talking about us."

"They won't have anything to talk about anymore soon. Come on, Ana. Let's go home."

"The stench in this slum is making me nauseous. That fat, useless whore can't even keep this place clean. Let's go home, Boris."

Once the door was shut behind them, she locked it and returned to the bedroom. Wrapped in the bedspread, Greg crawled back in from the fire escape.

"Man, that was a real trip!"

"I'm so sorry, Greg."

"It's not your fault. Your parents are totally looney-tunes. Interesting, how they stuck to English when they thought there was a man hiding and listening."

"I was afraid of something like this happening and scaring you away."

"It couldn't scare me away. I happen to be partial to women with loose morals." he kissed her.

"You're being very nice about this."

"'I smell a naked man.'? What does a naked man smell like? Where does she come up with this stuff?"

"I don't know about other naked men, but this one smells terrific."

"You smell pretty terrific yourself." he opened her robe and let it fall to the floor.

* * *

"There's so much noise upstairs, Blanche. It's making me awfully nervous." Ethel was searching through my cupboards for anything containing alcohol, "Don't you have any liquor, Blanche?"

"I'll get you some Nescafe."

"That just makes me more nervous. I need a drink."

"You'll be just fine, Ethel. Tell me what's wrong."

"Your little friend is quite the vixen, like they say in my stories."

"What are you talking about?"

"She's having sex with that Greg fellow."

"Good for her."

"Is that all you've got to say?"

"I'm happy for her. She deserves some happiness."

"Those two are making an awful lot of racket up there, what, with their carryings on, and her parents bawling her out about her activities, and Myrtle cursing at them...I can't watch my stories with so much going on...They spent last weekend going at it around the clock. They're up there after she gets home from work until he has to go to his job."

"I imagine it's the only time they're both free."

"She's not the prim and proper girl she makes on she is."

"I'm glad she's found someone. Nadya's been very lonely for a very long time. I don't think she's ever had a proper relationship before."

"There's nothing proper about this one, either."

"She's thirty-eight. She deserves some happiness."

"I suppose she's making up for lost time." Ethel laughed.

"This is the seventies, Ethel. The decade of free love."

"Free love, my foot." she turned on my television set, "Why don't we watch "Laugh-In"?"

"I'm up for that."

"I hope Richard Dawson's on it tonight. He makes me swoon."

"I'm not too fussy about him." I said, "The one I like is Peter Marshall from "Hollywood Squares". Now, he's a class act."

Chapter 6/ Mustard And Teal

The petite blonde in the ice-blue Orlon turtleneck and navy blue polyester pants took a seat at a table by the rain-streaked window. Outside, cars were swishing by, splashing the vexed pedestrians.

"What will you have?" Mama Rosa appeared at her table, smiling broadly.

"Oh, hello." she turned around and smiled back, "Just some hot chocolate, please."

"Good choice for a day like this. You don't have a coat, dear. You'll get soaked."

"My coat's upstairs in my apartment. I was doing some cleaning before I move in. I'm on a break."

"That's lovely news! Welcome to our Splendid. I think you'll like it here."

"Thank you. I know I will."

"It's wonderful to have a classy lady like you amongst us."

"Thank you." her smile was warm and earnest; her hair fell in soft waves around her un-made-up face.

"I'm Rosa, as in Mama Rosa." the plump woman in the red and white uniform extended her hand.

"I'm Joyce Field." she shook her hand, "I'm very pleased to meet you."

"I'll bring your hot chocolate over, along with a complimentary dessert of your choice."

"Oh, please." she protested.

"You name your favorite dessert and I'll bring it to you. Mama Rosa never takes no for an answer."

"In that case, I'll have the apple pie, please."

"A la mode?"

"Why not?"

"Coming right up."

Joyce returned to observing the goings on outside. A young couple came running toward the building, laughing. The young man was holding a black umbrella over the young woman's head, his free arm protectively encircling her. He opened the door adjacent to the restaurant door. The umbrella refused to close or fit through the door. The young woman's shoulder-length hair was plastered to her head. Her cardigan and dress were drenched. The young man's jeans were splashed with mud and his transparent white shirt clung to his chest hair. She smiled at their youthful innocence. A station wagon with wood panels drove by slowly, reversed, and came to a stop in front of the building. A Crown Victoria, which had been coasting behind it, paused briefly and resumed its slow pace.

"Here you are. I hope you enjoy it." Mama Rosa returned with her hot chocolate and pie.

"Thank you. The pie looks scrumptious." she smiled and resumed her people-watching.

There was no sign of the station wagon now. People in trench coats were walking briskly. The restaurant was filling up with more customers. A middle-aged brunette with a severe Madam haircut took a seat at a nearby table, removed her expensive-looking trench coat and placed it on an empty chair. She had on a mustard –colored turtleneck, a dangling gold pendant, and a black and white hound's-tooth pencil skirt. She produced a pair of reading glasses, a steno notebook and a pen from her pocketbook. When a young waiter promptly appeared at her table, she ordered Chicken Cacciatore and white wine.

The young couple from earlier burst in through the door connecting the restaurant to the apartment lobby, still laughing. They had removed their rain-soaked clothes and changed into more casual attire. The tall, striking man was in a new pair of jeans and a grey fisherman's pullover. The young woman was dressed in one of his sweaters – a black Fair Isle that nearly reached her knees. She had bare legs and a pair of oversized men's sneakers. She was self-consciously tugging at the sweater to cover more of her legs. Her towel-dried hair was fluffy like a little girl's.

"Well, hello!" Mama Rosa greeted them with familiarity, "Got caught in the rain, did you?"

"Doesn't she look adorable in my sweater and sneakers?" he said, "Mama Rosa, can we have your biggest pizza with everything on it, please?"

"Of course you can. What would you like to drink?"

"A beer for me and a Fresca for the lovely lady."

"Coming right up." she showed them to a table.

The woman in the mustard turtleneck, whose eyes had been on this couple, put on her reading glasses and began writing furiously in her notebook. Joyce's attention was soon diverted to a new and boisterous presence: An extremely overweight, middle-aged woman in a teal green sporty rain jacket and teal stretch pants was laughing loudly and embracing numerous men at nearby tables. She chose a table near the young couple and cast a complacent glance toward them. She had the type of disc-shaped brown eyes Joyce had often observed on women of dubious character. The woman's bleached hair was cut in an unflattering straight mid-ear style. She ordered spaghetti and meatballs and red wine, batting her short eyelashes at the young waiter.

"Can I get you anything else, dear?" Mama Rosa was back at Joyce's table.

"I wouldn't mind another hot chocolate." she said, "Very cute young couple over there."

"They live here in the building. He's a police officer and she's a bookkeeper. I'll be back with your hot chocolate."

Joyce attempted to meet Mustard's gaze, however, the woman looked away and guzzled her wine. Teal continued ogling the cute couple. The man cast a menacing glance in Teal's direction. When his companion excused herself, Teal wasted no time approaching him.

"Hi, Greg. Looking sexy as always."

"Sling your hook, Gwen." he retorted.

"If you get tired of playing kindergarten, you know where to find me."

"No thanks."

"Sooner or later, you'll get tired of Miss Goody-Two-Shoes and need a real woman who can meet your needs."

"I already have a real woman and all my needs are met."

"She'd never do the things for you that I would...If you want to sample the wares, you know where to find me."

"I'm not interested in anything you have to offer, Gwen." the man pulled his companion who had just returned into an embrace.

"You must be an old pro in bed to keep this stud muffin satisfied." Gwen smirked and made an attempt to step toward the younger woman.

"Get lost, Gwen." Greg commanded.

"You know where I am if you change your mind." she winked at him and padded back to her own table.

"In your dreams, freak." he shot back at her.

"Who is that woman?" his companion asked.

"A psycho. Forget about her." he reassured her.

Back at her table, Teal continued to eye Greg with a smirk. Mustard, who had been observing Teal with disdain, put away her notebook, pen and reading glasses. She motioned to her waiter to bring her the check and requested that he place the remainder of her meal in a take-out container. On her way out, she made a point of brushing past the couple's table.

Joyce ordered Fettuccini Alfredo and a Tab soda. She intended to remain there until the couple consumed their meal without more harassment from Teal or anyone else. She was prepared to intervene, if necessary. Nobody was going to harm these lovely young people. Not on her watch.

Chapter 7/ A Matter Of Honor

The park was resplendent with yellow flowers and birdsong. Hands linked, they walked to the bandstand which was painted a loud shade of turquoise.

"I loved looking at your family photos." she said, "A big Irish family, lots of siblings, a huge Victorian house...It's like a storybook to me."

"Some of the mischief my brothers and I got into was nothing out of a storybook." he laughed, his dimples deepening, "I'd like us to have our own storybook family album."

"There's nothing I'd like more." her head was resting on his shoulder.

"Why don't we spend next weekend in Saints' Harbor with my folks?"

"Your folks wouldn't exactly be thrilled if you showed up with me."

"Why not?"

"I'm not exactly the kind of woman you'd take home to meet your parents, Greg."

"They'd love you."

"If you were my son, I wouldn't want you to bring home someone like me."

"They gave up trying to tell me how to live my life long ago. At forty-three, they know I'm old enough to know what's best for me."

"I wouldn't want to be the cause of a rift between you and your parents, Greg. They wouldn't want to see you with an outcast. I'm damaged goods."

"You're perfect for me."

"You're the one who's perfect." she stroked his hair, "They'd want you with someone from a wholesome, loving, stable family, someone who survived all rites of passage with minimal damage, someone who was nurtured and encouraged to follow her dreams, surrounded by a supportive, caring social network...A happy, well-adjusted, successful, popular, capable woman who is also young enough to give you children."

"This fictional woman sounds awfully boring." he raised his eyebrows.

"That's the type of woman most men want to build a future with."

"Not this one. That's why I'm still single at forty-three. I didn't want to settle the way other guys did. No one was the right fit until I met you."

"No one was ever right for me until I met you."

"I've already told the folks I have a very special lady in my life. They want to meet you."

"They're in for a disappointment."

"They're going to love you."

"I'm sure they'd want grandchildren."

"They might get their wish." he patted her abdomen, "We haven't been taking any precautions."

"At my age, there could be complications. The night of our first time, I had every intention of using preventative measures, but when I saw you, I threw all caution to the wind. I've been terrified of losing you if I ended up pregnant."

"Losing me? Baby or no baby, I'm afraid you're stuck with me. We're going to have one of these Victorian houses right here overlooking this park. We can start our own storybook."

"This is all like a fairy tale to me, Greg. I'm terrified I might wake up and discover you never really existed."

They sat in each other's arms, unaware of the young man in the forest green Datsun taking their photographs.

* * *

The rain was beating down against the window. Her face was buried in his chest, her favorite spot, her safe place. He was stroking her hair.

"I could hold you like this forever, Nadya."

"I wish you could."

"I waited so long to let you know how I felt about you. I was afraid to make a move. You were so fragile...like a sparrow with a broken wing. I didn't dare touch you because I thought you might break into a thousand pieces."

"I was already broken, Greg. You put me back together."

He blinked away his tears and kissed her forehead.

* * *

The freckled young woman with the red pixie cut leaned her back against the fire escape railing and slipped her hands into the pockets of her uniform pants.

"This Walter Messer guy swears up and down he lost control of the car when he dropped a contact lens and bent down to look for it."

"We can't charge him with anything more than dangerous driving." Greg sighed and rolled his eyes, "I know her parents put that mother fucker up to it, to scare her into celibacy. Five minutes with him, and I'd get him to sing like a canary."

"That's why the boss wants you out of it. You're too emotionally involved." the young woman said, "You'd lose your temper and get yourself into trouble. Don't worry, partner. I'll do a thorough job."

"I don't doubt that, Lesley Anne. I just hate having my hands tied."

"I understand. You're in love with her. You want to protect her. You want to make all of this go away."

"And that Hortense is a real piece of work."

"She is. She claims that, about twenty-four years ago, Boris Babayevski told her and other colleagues a sob story about having a wild child for a daughter. He said he and his wife couldn't handle her. She was an out-of-control, boy-crazy teenager. He told

Hortense that, in their culture, girls were not permitted to go anywhere or speak to anyone without a chaperone, but his daughter was breaking all the rules and running all over town. He and his wife were beside themselves and needed someone to follow their daughter and report back to them."

"And Hortense thought this was acceptable?"

"She said she felt very sorry for him, trying to uphold his heritage, but having so much trouble with his rebellious daughter. She volunteered to play detective."

Greg was pacing the floor, gritting his teeth.

"At thirty-eight, Nadya can hardly be considered a teenager!" Mel laughed.

"Supposedly, any unmarried daughter of any age must be watched and followed closely to be kept in line, or she will be considered a source of great shame for the family. Hortense said she had tremendous respect for a man trying to maintain his family's honor."

"What a pile of bullshit!" Greg shouted, "What, according to Madame Hortense, was the 'wild child' doing that was so appalling? Did she tell you what she observed during her snooping sessions?"

"Apparently, she was walking home from school with some girls from welfare families after she had been warned by her parents to stay away from them."

"Perish the thought. How immoral." Mel shook his head.

"She also spied her sitting on the school steps, waiting for the bus, reading, and talking with some boys. I asked if there was any behavior to suggest flirtation, and she admitted it all appeared platonic. No hand holding, teasing, kissing, or physical contact. However, the fact that she was having any type of dialogue with boys, under any circumstances, was not permitted by her parents. I asked if she ever observed her going to inappropriate places. Again, no: Only record stores, book stores and the library. And always by herself."

“And, every time that old bag reported to her parents, Nadya was beaten, berated and tortured.” Greg’s eyes were welling up with tears.

“How do any of these activities define a wild child?” Mel asked.

“There was an attempt at an arranged marriage at one time, and I guess Nadya objected. That got her labelled as a spiteful, rebellious ingrate.”

“Didn’t this Hortense ever go to work, home, or anywhere else normal people do? Did she play amateur sleuth around the clock?”

“Apparently, she contracted out. Her family, friends and neighbors picked up the slack. They all thought it was fun and exciting.”

“Filthy, sick mother fuckers!” Greg banged his fist against the wall, “I remember Nadya telling me, when she was in university, her parents were so paranoid, her mother signed up for the same courses as hers, to keep a constant eye on her. She only had one boyfriend, and he had to cross-dress when they went out in public.”

“You might have to start doing the same, Greg.” Lesley Anne smirked, “I can take you shopping for some cute outfits.”

“You’d look foxy in a mini skirt.” Mel winked.

“Nadya’s terrified of her parents.” Greg said, “Those sadistic bastards have been torturing her all her life, imprisoning her as their personal slave and punching bag. She’s been forcefully confined, beaten, berated, and gaslighted all these years...She said no man wanted to be near her because she was so damaged...She’s been so lonely all her life.”

“Now, she has you. Please don’t ever hurt her, Greg.” Lesley Anne said, “I don’t think she would survive if you abandoned her.”

“I would never do that, Lesley Anne.” Greg said, tears glistening in his eyes, “I plan to be by her side to my dying day.”

* * *

“I think this is the last of your stuff, Miss Field.” the blond man placed a mover’s box on top of another one in her kitchen.

“Miss Field? Jim, we practically grew up together! You were Hazel’s baby brother. You called me Joyce back then.”

“You were a kid then.”

“Sometimes, I think I still am.” she opened her pocketbook, produced a check book, and began writing a check on top of one of the stacks of boxes with the pen from the countertop, “Give my best to Mary Jane and the kids.”

“Certainly will.”

Through the open apartment door, they heard raised voices down the hall.

“Sounds like you’ve got some loud neighbors.” Jim remarked.

“I’ll go check things if it doesn’t quiet down soon.” she handed him the check.

“That’s not a good idea. It could be dangerous. You should probably call the cops.”

“I don’t want to get my neighbors into trouble.”

“I don’t know. It sounds pretty bad. Why don’t you let me check for you?”

“If it’s a volatile situation, I don’t want to put you in danger, Jim.”

“That’s okay.” he started down the hall.

“Let’s go together, then.” she followed him.

“Hello? Is everybody okay in there?” Jim knocked firmly.

“Get out of here!” a man with a heavy accent answered from behind the closed door.

“Sir, please open the door.” Joyce said.

“I told you to get out of here! This doesn’t concern you.” the man retorted, “This is a family matter. Now, get the hell out of here!”

“We’d better leave.” Jim whispered.

An exasperated Joyce followed Jim, sighing.

“Whose apartment is that?” Jim asked.

“I don’t know. I haven’t met any of the neighbors yet.”

“I don’t think this is a safe place for you to live, Joyce.”

“I’ll be fine, Jim. I’m sure it was just a small family squabble.”

"I hate to leave you alone like this. Make sure you lock your door."

"Don't worry, Jim. I'll be fine."

"I hope your other neighbors are friendlier." he put on his cap, "You take it easy now."

"Thanks for moving me."

"Any time."

Jim passed a striking brunette on the stairs and nodded in greeting. She smiled congenially.

"Hello." the brunette said to Joyce, "You must be the new neighbor. I'm Olivia Cordova."

"I'm Joyce Field. Nice to meet you."

"Nice to meet you, too. Welcome to The Splendid." Olivia turned her key in the lock, "Tell you what: Why don't you come to my apartment? We can order a pizza from downstairs and have it delivered. I've got some red wine."

"I'd like that." Joyce picked up her pocketbook from the kitchen table, checked for her keys inside and locked her door behind her.

Olivia deposited her briefcase on the floor beside her hall table and hung her pocketbook from a hook. The menacing voices from the altercation next door were clearly audible. Olivia noticed the solicitude on Joyce's face.

"I'm used to it by now." she smiled, "I share a wall with her apartment, so I get an earful."

"Do they do this on a regular basis?"

"Fairly regularly. It's been worse these last couple of months since Nadya started dating Greg."

The cute couple from the restaurant, Joyce thought.

"Who are the ones arguing with her?"

"Her parents."

"Why don't they approve of him?"

"It's not him in particular. They wouldn't approve of Prince Charles if he were dating their daughter. They want her under their control."

"Very disturbing family dynamics."

"I'm so glad she has Greg to protect her now."

"My mover and I tried to intervene earlier, but they wouldn't open the door. The man was belligerent with us."

"There's no use trying to intervene. They'll just take it out on her. Some of the neighbors have called the police in the past. It only made things worse for Nadya."

"That poor young woman."

"I think Greg has reached his breaking point. He might do something drastic to keep them away from her."

"Drastic measures might be necessary in this case."

"I think they're leaving." Olivia whispered, "I heard the door open."

They strained their ears to listen to the footsteps past Olivia's door and down the stairs. Tiptoeing next door, they knocked softly.

"Nadya, are you all right?" Olivia called out.

The door was opened, and Nadya stood, her face pale, her eyes dead, her hair falling away from a loose ponytail.

"Oh, honey..." Olivia embraced her.

Joyce instinctively reached out to hold her.

"It's going to be all right, sweetheart. They're never going to hurt you again, I promise."

And, in that maternal warmth, Nadya found it safe to release the torrent of tears she had been holding back for so long.

* * *

The day Sandra moved in, Joyce was the first one to welcome her. Soon, Olivia and Arlene joined her.

"I appreciate your warm welcome. I would love to have coffee with all of you tomorrow afternoon at the restaurant downstairs."

"It's so nice to have you for a neighbor." Arlene said.

"Likewise."

"There was supposed to be a new neighbor next to your apartment, too, but no one's moved in yet."

"That's my friend Vince. He'll be here in two weeks. He's tying up loose ends with his Rosedale Contessa."

"What does that mean?" Arlene asked.

"My friend is a magnet for narcissistic socialites."

"Elmdale has its share of those, too." Arlene said, "I grew up on the poor end of Waterloo Row. The girls from the rich end and from all the streets off Waterloo were so stuck up, even now, after twenty-five years, they act all condescending around me when they come into the shop to get their hair done."

"Snobs make me break out in a rash." Sandra said, "Every place has them, but, for the most part, Elmdale seems to be a pleasant place. It's a welcome change after so many years of crime fighting in Toronto. I like it here already now that I know I have neighbors like you."

"Welcome to Splendid Hotel." Olivia hugged her.

A well-dressed older couple came up the stairs. Without a nod of acknowledgement to any of them, they marched to the end of the hallway, and began banging on Nadya's door.

"Excuse me." Arlene intercepted them, "Nadya isn't home."

"Where is she?"

"I wouldn't know that, sir."

"She got off work an hour ago. She should be here."

"Maybe she's buying groceries." Arlene said.

Myrtle came stomping up the stairs.

"Youse two lookin' for your daughter?"

"Yes we are."

"I'll show youse where she is. Shacked up with that cop right across the hall from me."

Olivia and Joyce exchanged glances, cringing. Arlene turned beet red and lowered her eyes.

"Are they in there now?"

"You bet your sweet bippy they are. Youse better break it up. They're creating a disturbance. They go at it every afternoon like jackals in heat."

"What are those two going to do, call a cop?" Arlene whispered.

"I'd better warn them." Olivia whispered, "I'll call Greg's number." She ran into her apartment.

"This must be a very interesting place to live." Sandra remarked.

"You ain't seen nothin' yet." Arlene winked.

"Can't wait." she said with a bemused smile.

"He picked it up, so he's expecting the wild banshees to descend upon them." Olivia returned.

"They must have heard the wild banshees from here and lost the mood anyway." Arlene smiled mischievously.

Loud voices and banging from downstairs were clearly audible.

"I knew you were hiding a man in your apartment that time! Looks like you moved the side show to another location. No wonder we can't reach you anymore! You've been living in sin with this man for weeks. Get dressed right now and get up the stairs to your apartment, where we can deal with this."

"This is my apartment, and I would like you to leave." Greg was standing, wrapped in his plaid bedspread, shielding Nadya, who was covering herself with a bedsheet, "You are completely out of line in the way you treat your daughter."

"Are you going to let this rough uncle speak to us this way? We are your parents, and we're only trying to protect you. Look at the way you let men use you shamelessly! They're all laughing at you behind your back. None of them care about you. None of them value you or respect you."

"You're going to have to leave now. Nadya is not going anywhere with you."

"You're going to regret this, Nadya. He's going to throw you away, just like the others."

"Is their daughter under age?" Sandra asked.

"She'll be thirty-nine in a few weeks. She's still the youngest one in the building."

"Then, I don't understand why it's such a state of emergency if she is involved with a man, and obviously a very respectable man."

"Strange family dynamics." Joyce remarked.

"I'll say. I haven't run across anything this bizarre, even in twenty-five years of police work in a city like Toronto."

"I'm sorry this had to happen on your moving day." Arlene said.

"That's all right. What worries me is, your friend could be in danger of getting evicted if anyone complained about the ruckus her parents are creating."

"That's what her parents probably want." Olivia said, "They want her back home under their thumb, so they can have complete control over her life."

"That poor young woman. This is serious abuse."

"We all try to look out for her. All except Myrtle, that is, the one you just saw." Arlene said.

"Ethel's not too fond of her, either, but Blanche keeps Ethel in line. Blanche is like a mother to all of us." Olivia said.

"I'm looking forward to meeting Blanche, as well as Greg and...sorry, I didn't catch your friend's name."

"Nadya."

"What a beautiful name."

* * *

"They treat me like I'm retarded." Nadya was curled up in a ball in Greg's bed, "Maybe I am."

"Nadya, you can't let them get to you like this, sweetheart." he held her stiff body, "You know they're trying to break you by playing sadistic mind games with you."

"Maybe they are right. Maybe I really am defective and repulsive and a laughing stock."

"Those assholes! I could strangle them! Nadya, don't listen to that crap! They're jealous because you're living your life without them and thriving."

"Maybe I really am just a joke. Greg, until I met you, all men treated me with contempt and ridicule. If you only knew all the things men have done to me for so long..."

"They weren't men. They were scum."

"You don't have to feel you have to stay with me out of pity, Greg. I am not going to get all clingy and weepy. You can walk away from me any time you want."

"Nadya, I would rather cut off my right arm than leave you or do anything to hurt you. I am always going to love you."

"I am always going to love you, too, Greg."

"I'm going to make us something to eat." he arranged the covers around her, "But, first, there's a song I want you to hear. I heard it on the radio on my way to work. The lyrics blew me away. It could've been written about you. I went out and bought the record. It's "Wildflower" by a group called Skylark." he kissed her forehead and turned on the phonograph, placing the needle on the song, "It was originally a poem written by a cop about his girlfriend."

She reached out for his hands, kissed both of them and pressed them to her cheeks.

Chapter 8/ Family

Coming up the stairs, she could hear Johnny Hartman singing "My One And Only Love" on the phonograph. Greg opened his door and pulled her into an embrace.

"Aren't you a sight for sore eyes?" he kissed her.

"I love coming home to you."

"How would you like to come home to me every day for the rest of our lives?"

Her eyes widened in astonishment as he reached into his pocket and produced a small gift-wrapped package tied with a pink ribbon.

"Nadya, will you marry me?"

"Oh, Greg, yes, yes! I'll marry you!"

He placed the diamond solitaire on her finger.

"Nothing can ever tear us apart." he held her.

"Nothing and no one."

* * *

Greg parked the car in front of an ornate brownstone with curved windows. She glanced around the gracious street with elegant heritage homes. He led her up the walkway with an arm around her. The door was opened before they reached the top of the front steps, and an older couple emerged with outstretched arms. All of her fears and doubts vanished at that moment.

"Here she is, Ma." Greg said, "My Nadya."

"Welcome to the family, dear." his mother hugged her, "I'm Eileen."

"It's so nice to meet you."

"My husband, Patrick." she turned to the man beside her.

Nadya shook his hand.

"You've done good, son." the man kissed her cheek, as Greg hugged Eileen.

"Good to see you, Pop."

Entering the grand hall of this welcoming home, she was filled with warmth. The rich woodwork, the timeless, classic furnishings were unlike any home she had known. This was a real home, well-loved by a real family.

A woman who appeared slightly older than herself ran out to the hallway to greet her.

"Hi, I'm Doreen. I've been dying to meet the woman who finally tamed our wild child. Never thought we'd see the day."

"Keep that bad boy in line." a male voice called out from the parlor.

"That's my brother Shawn." Doreen said.

With Greg on one side and Doreen on the other, she entered the double parlor where the family was assembled, occupying every square inch of space.

"This is my brother Patrick," Greg began the introductions, "And his lovely wife Maureen. He's a cop, too, and she's a florist. This is my brother, Shawn, another cop. We followed in Pop's footsteps. This is Shawn's lovely wife Mary. She runs a daycare center. This is my brother Joe. He's a probation officer. And here's Carol, his lovely wife, a social worker."

"Law enforcement is in your blood."

"This is my husband Ken." Doreen said, "We're both probation officers. This is our sister Joan. She's a legal assistant like Mom. Her husband Tom is a guard at the local jail. And, of course, the baby of the family: Miss Kathleen. She's a dance instructor."

"Very nice to meet all of you."

"We're very happy to meet you, Nadya."

"They'd all given up hope on me settling down." Greg exchanged jovial smiles with his brothers.

"This must be overwhelming for you, Nadya." Doreen said, "So many of us all in one room."

"I think it's wonderful that you have each other. You're never alone. There's a whole family that will always look out for you."

"Wait till you get to know this noisy clan. You'll wonder what you got yourself into." Joan said.

"This house was a three-ring circus when we were growing up." Kathleen laughed, "The boys were always beating the crap out of each other."

"The boys were always in hot water." Joan said, "And, of course, Greg was the instigator every time."

"I wasn't that bad. What are you trying to do? Scare her away?"

"Admit it: You were the black sheep of the family." Patrick said.

"I'm beginning to think it was a bad idea to introduce you to Nadya. You're trying to scare her away."

"I'm not easy to scare."

"That's a good thing, 'cause we've got all sorts of stories to tell you about him." Joe said.

Greg was turning red and laughing nervously.

"But we all look back upon those days with so much fondness." Kathleen said.

"We're a package deal." Joan said, "When you marry Greg, you get stuck with the rest of us, too."

"I'm going to enjoy that."

"Wait till you meet all the grandkids." Doreen said, "They're all playing upstairs. You're going to have a huge brood of nieces and nephews."

"Greg got all the girls when we were growing up." Shawn said, "He had the good looks, the shy smile, the impish charm."

"Don't listen to them." Greg said.

After dinner, all the women retreated into the enormous country style kitchen. Greg's brothers crowded around him in the parlor. His dad patted him on the back.

"I'm happy for you, son."

* * *

"You must be worn out from all the commotion, dear." Eileen placed an arm around her, "Now that everyone else has gone home,

I'll show you to your room. We'll have a proper visit, just the four of us, tomorrow."

"Thank you. That would be nice."

"I've got Greg's old room set up for the two of you. If there's anything you need, let me know."

Eileen was amused by the look of astonishment on Nadya's face.

"You're not teenagers." Eileen said with a wink, "I know my son. He'd never forgive me if I put you in separate rooms. He'd be sneaking into your room anyway, so make yourselves at home, dear. I'm very pleased Greg's met a nice girl like you."

* * *

Mel found him slumped over in his chair, tears streaming down his cheeks.

"Hey, pal, it's going to be okay." he patted him on the back.

"She was coming back from the doctor's office. A car went up on the sidewalk and hit her from behind."

"I've got the licence number from two witnesses. We'll get 'im."

"How many more of them are there? It's like a hornet's nest. As soon as you get one, there's a thousand more."

"We'll get 'em all."

"She was pregnant. She lost the baby."

"I'm so sorry, pal. Is she going to be all right?"

"They said there are no internal injuries. She'll be sore and bruised for a while. They sedated her." he gazed lovingly at her sleeping, "When I get my hands on who did this, he won't know what hit him!"

"Leave that to us, Greg. You concentrate on her."

"I've filed a formal complaint with your dad against Myrtle. She was doing our heads in. She's like a venomous snake."

"Smart move. It's about time someone stood up to that trouble-maker. She's been hounding Dad about you guys and your loud bedroom activities." he winked.

"She's let us know on no uncertain terms she disapproves of us." Greg said, "When we're in Nadya's apartment, Myrtle bangs on her bedroom ceiling with a broom handle. When we're in my apartment, she stands outside the door, cursing. She's a real piece of work."

"She's been getting worse and worse."

"I've had it with those psycho parents of Nadya's, too. If they come around again, I'm getting a restraining order. That is the last thing she needs. If I find myself alone with those two assholes, I won't be responsible for my actions."

"With those two as her parents, it's a miracle Nadya turned out the way she did."

"She's a rare gem. And I intend to protect her from them."

"You've got a lot of vacation time coming, buddy. Take all the time you need."

"When you get that piece of scum who hit her, Mel, I want to be the one to interrogate him! This time, they went too far!"

"Greg, you know what Sergeant Fraser said: You're too emotionally involved."

"Mel, I want to be there to put the screws to that mother fucker! I want to know the name of the son of a bitch who hired him and the others!"

"Leave that to me and the guys. We'll get whoever is behind it. You need to stand back."

"Nothing doing. I want one of them to crack and tell me the name of the son of a bitch! I want to pulverize the bastards!"

"You need to concentrate on you and Nadya, and building your future."

"We may never be able to have children now. They took our child away from us!"

"You'll have the family both of you want."

"You know Nadya turned thirty-nine last week. We don't have a big window of opportunity."

"Lots of women have kids after forty. Nadya's youthful for her age. Her inner workings must be in good condition, too. I'm sure she's got a few good childbearing years ahead of her yet."

"We're not giving up."

"Take some time off and relax. You hang in there, buddy."

"Thanks, pal."

Nadya stirred and attempted to open her eyes.

"Greg?"

"I'm here, sweetheart." he squeezed her hand.

"I'm sorry about what happened, Nadya." Mel stepped closer, "We're going to catch them; don't worry."

"Thanks, Mel." she attempted to smile.

"I'm going to get on this now. You two hang in there. It's all going to be over soon." Mel closed the door softly as he left.

"How are you feeling?" Greg turned to her solicitously, "Are you in pain?"

"Just groggy. Seeing you beside me is the best medicine. Are you all right?"

"Never mind about me. I'm going to be by your side every minute of every day."

"I'm a lucky girl."

"I love you." he kissed her softly, "There's an officer posted outside the door at all times."

"And my favorite officer is right here beside me." she took his hand, "I wish you could lie next to me."

"I think they have cots they can put next to the bed. I'll ask for one. I'll be right beside you all night."

"As long as you're next to me, Greg, no one can hurt me – ever."

Chapter 9/ Obstacle Course

"I wonder when he is planning to tell her." Mel said.

"If he's waiting for her to get stronger, it's going to be a long wait." Gayle said, "Something like this is not easy to deal with. She's going to need a lot of time and support."

"She can't deal with this news on top of everything else." Olivia said.

"Interesting that her parents haven't shown up once since her accident." Joyce remarked, "Not even to show fake concern."

"I expected Ma and Pa Kettle to show up with their old cast-offs as gifts, showing fake concern." Olivia said, "In fact, I'm surprised they weren't even here for her birthday."

"I'm glad she was able to spend a nice quiet time with Greg on her birthday before the second accident." Joyce said.

"Ma and Pa Kettle might have something more sinister up their sleeves." Sandra said, "They've realized their lifelong aggressive, intimidating approach is no longer effective, because, for the first time, she has support from her friends, and most of all, she has a real significant other who is committed to her and cares about her. They're changing their tactics. I think some sort of a plan's been in the works since they first found her with Greg. They must be quite intimidated by him. He is strong and masculine, and a police officer, to boot. That must've shaken them to their core. Vince and I've been discussing this situation at length on the phone. We worked on cases about families like this for so long, I guess old habits die hard."

"We certainly appreciate your input, Sandra." Mel said, "When is Vince moving in, anyway?"

"Very soon. He's the nicest guy you'll ever meet, and the smartest, too, but he is always so humble."

"Are things all smoothed out with Penelope, the Rosedale Contessa?" Arlene asked.

"I'm afraid not. I'm just glad he's getting away from Toronto and its elite. He unfortunately attracts too much attention from certain types of women."

"We're all anxious to meet him." Mel said, "I hope you ladies can control yourselves when you do."

"There's no way to predict what their next move might be." Sandra said, "Her parents need to be under close scrutiny. Those hoodlums crying foul, claiming police brutality from Greg were coached by the head honcho. Her dad is after Greg's badge. People like that play dirty. Greg needs to watch his back."

"I had no idea they were capable of such heinous acts." Arlene said.

"We've seen this behavior in Toronto with families from repressive Middle-Eastern, South Asian and even East-European cultures like Nadya's. They more often than not end in tragedy. They want total control over their daughters, and recruit friends and relatives to follow their daughters everywhere to ensure that they have no contact with the opposite sex. In all the cases we've run across, the daughters were in their teens. If they showed the slightest interest in boys, they were tortured and beaten, and married off to old men. If the girls did not comply, they were murdered."

"Nadya's parents were always like this, but they kept her around as a punching bag and a slave. They seemed to enjoy watching her suffer. It's like a sick hobby. If they killed her, they wouldn't know what to do with themselves." Olivia said.

"They were trying to marry her off to old men when she was in her late teens. She defied them at every turn. She had her own mind and she put up with all sorts of crap without giving in to their demands. They're still trying to make her pay for being a 'rebel'." Arlene said, "I'm a couple of years older than she is, but I used to see her around town and we'd talk. She turned a lot of heads. All older men. They were too intimidated by her stunning beauty to ever ask her out. She assumed they didn't find her attractive. Boys our age were mean to her. She was always by herself, always so sad."

"With her horrendous home life, she must've had a hard time keeping herself together." Joyce said, "When she was younger, her parents likely held out hope that they'd eventually break her spirit completely and she'd comply with their wishes. They perhaps hoped to marry her off to a wealthy man and benefit from it themselves."

"Now that she's at an age that makes her less desirable to those older men, they might think of her as a liability." Sandra said, "This young woman is in grave danger."

"Man, this is heavy." Mel shook his head.

"Vince said this is beyond archaic Old World traditions. He mentioned Narcissistic Personality Disorder. Among a myriad of other defects, narcissists have an obsession with keeping up appearances. They crave attention and admiration from prestigious people. The standards they set for their children are completely unrealistic and superficial. Any offspring who do not live up to their standards are rejected. Narcissists have no capacity for empathy, compassion, love, or remorse. It's all about them. They are not beyond murdering an adult child if they feel they have been shamed by their behavior."

"I wish Vince were here." Mel said, "He could really help us crack this case."

"He'll be here soon. He's quite intrigued by this situation." Sandra said, "I never imagined that, when we moved here to pursue new careers, we'd be doing what we left behind."

"Being a cop is in your blood forever." Mel said, "I don't think Greg needs to know all this just yet. He's in a very bad place right now. He's drinking heavily and he'll do something impetuous, get himself hurt or in more trouble. He's already on a six month suspension. He could lose his job if he doesn't behave himself. I'm worried about his health – his physical and mental health both. He needs to get away and clear his head."

"Very tragic." Joyce said.

"The Staff Sergeant told him a while back he wanted him off the case because he was too emotionally involved. He refused to back off. Then, he got a little carried away interrogating the lowlife scum. He got hit with a police brutality complaint. He lost it and started punching walls and knocking over desks. He's been ordered to get psychological counselling."

"This is so sad." Gayle said, "Falling in love's been a painful journey for him. He used to be a love 'em and leave 'em ladies' man, couldn't settle down with one woman. Nadya was not the type of woman I thought he'd fall for. I could see him hitting on her, sure, but the way this has played out really boggles my mind."

"Obviously, there's more to him than meets the eye." Mel said.

"He's an intense, complex young man." Joyce said, "Nadya is a very complex person, too. I truly feel for them. They deserve to live their lives in a safe, happy environment. Both of them are so endearing, so earnest, and so much in love, anyone who'd want to hurt them would have to be a monster."

* * *

The smoky strains of "Here, There, And Everywhere" was on the phonograph. She was gazing adoringly at his handsome face in the lethargic outdoor bulb of the fire escape. His smoldering dark green eyes met her gaze and he pulled her into a tearful kiss. She unbuttoned his shirt and planted feverish kisses on his chest.

"Wait here." she whispered and entered the building through the fire exit.

The ailing light bulb was put out of its misery. She returned to the darkened fire escape and his arms. Her mouth explored every pore on his body. She fell to her knees and took him in her mouth. He stifled his moans in the humid night air.

"What did I ever do to deserve you?" he knelt down, pulled her dress over his head and buried his face in her.

When they climbed back into her apartment through the window, the lights across the river were slowly dimming. He went out to the hallway to turn the exterior light back on. With trembling fingers, he poured himself a drink of bourbon in the kitchen. She placed her reassuring hand over his.

* * *

"Do you remember Gwen?" the freckled young woman was smiling mischievously.

"Gwen." he frowned.

"Gwen the social worker."

"Oh her." he grimaced.

"Well, guess whose name came up when we ran some of those licence plates?"

"You're putting me on!"

"Gwendolyn Giles. She's one of the culprits."

"Holy shit! That doesn't even make sense! What connection would she have to Nadya?"

"The green-eyed monster." she said, "I remember this woman coming on to you pretty strong on many occasions."

"Man, oh man, I can't believe this! She was an obnoxious, pushy, creepy old floozy."

"And she happened to be carrying a torch for you. She didn't take your rejection well."

"How did she get entangled in this?" his expressive eyebrows were raised quizzically.

"Greg, this is a small town. It wouldn't have been hard for her to find out about her parents and to ingratiate herself to them."

"Man, oh man! Damn it!" he punched the side of a filing cabinet.

"She's a social worker. She has access to all the files at the clinic. Nadya received some counselling there after her sexual assault twenty years ago. It wouldn't be hard for Gwen to snoop through Dr. Nelson's files and get personal information about her."

"This is getting way too weird, man! Is she the head honcho, the mastermind?"

"Nothing is for certain yet. Greg, you've got to step away and leave this in our hands. We'll do right by Nadya. I'm worried about you."

"I appreciate that, Lesley Anne. By the way, can you do me a favor?"

"Sure."

"Can you drive Nadya home? I don't think she'll be able to get herself home when she comes out of Fraser's office."

"Sure thing." she smiled.

"And, Lesley Anne, can you make sure she's not alone? Can you ask the lady in Apartment 7 to stay with her? Her name's Olivia."

"No problem."

When Nadya emerged from the Staff Sergeant's office with red, puffy eyes, Greg led her into an interrogation room for privacy.

"Everything's going to be all right, sweetie." he held her, "No one's ever done anything like this for me before. You're my angel."

"I'm sorry it didn't work."

"That doesn't matter, honey. This is just temporary. I'll get my head shrunk and clean up my act, get down on my knees and kiss their feet...They'll take me back."

"Where are you going?"

"I'm driving up to my uncle's cabin to do some fishing, meditating and soul searching. He's got a temporary job lined up for me in Hub City as a bouncer, starting in three weeks."

"You take good care of yourself."

"Don't worry about me. I'll be fine. You're all that matters."

"I've messed up your life, Greg. You would've been so much better off if you'd never met me."

"Nadya, you are the best thing that ever happened to me or will ever happen to me. I'm a far better man because of knowing you."

"You wouldn't be suspended now."

"It's no big deal. I don't want you to worry, sweetheart. I'm a big boy."

"I love you so much, Greg."

"And I love you, madly, totally, my beautiful Nadya."

"I can't live without you."

"When you look at me with those innocent eyes, I just want us to leave everything behind and take off to live like gypsies...sleep under the stars..."

"I've caused you so much pain, Greg."

"You've given me more love than I ever imagined possible...Nadya, I would do it all again in a heartbeat. I wouldn't trade what we had for anything in the world." he held her close, "I love you. I'm always going to love you. You and I are always going to be a part of each other...Sweetheart, please don't cry...I'm going to start crying, too, and you know, if these tough guys see me crying, I'll never hear the end of it."

She lifted her eyes to his face and stroked his cheek.

"I can't get out of here yet, but I'll see you at home as soon as I get my stuff cleared out." he kissed her cheek, "My partner's going to drive you home." he led her out to the hallway with an arm around her.

Lesley Anne approached them.

"Hi. I'm Greg's partner, Lesley Anne Norris." she shook Nadya's hand, "I feel like I know you already. Greg's talked so much about you. I'm very happy he's met you."

"He's suspended because of me. It's so unfair." Nadya said once they were in the squad car.

"It's not your fault. He'll be all right. In six months, he'll be rejuvenated and ready to go after the bad guys again. The time off will do him good."

"Thank you."

"Greg's been like a big brother to me. He's stood up for me when the other guys were either being chauvinistic jerks or hitting on me."

"That's the kind of guy he is."

"He's worried about you. I'd like you to feel free to call me any time while he's away."

Lesley Anne led a red-eyed Nadya up the stairs to the third floor hallway of The Splendid, where a small group was congregated. Her uniformed presence caused them to tense up.

"Nothing to worry about, folks." she smiled, "Is one of you called Olivia?"

"I am." Olivia stepped forward.

"Greg would like you to stay with Nadya until he gets home. He doesn't want her to be alone."

"Of course." Olivia placed her arm around Nadya.

"Thank you, Officer Norris." Nadya said.

"Lesley Anne, please. Take care of yourself and don't hesitate to call me." she waved on her way down the stairs.

Chapter 10/ Ravaged

And he was gone. There was nothing but silence. That familiar abyss threatened to swallow her up once again. She missed the scent of his skin, the taste of his body, the touch of his hands. Her body ached for his. With great happiness, there was the inevitable grief that followed after the source of happiness was taken away.

She was back in the dungeon of her former life. The terror of revisiting that torture was a fate far worse than death.

Each day after work, she retreated into her apartment and pushed a chest of drawers in front of her door. She made a point of not turning on her television, radio, cassette player, or phonograph, to give the illusion of not being home. She did not answer the phone or the door for anyone. She did not turn on her lights after dark. She slid under the covers and listened to the tortured strains of jazz standards from across the hall in the evenings. She cried until she fell asleep from exhaustion. She wanted Greg to be healed from the turmoil she had caused him and to have equilibrium restored in his life. He had been the only person to make her a priority, and her priority was his well-being. His face was before her every moment of every day...his impish grin, his dimples, his expressive eyebrows, his enormous dark green eyes...

Someone or some people out there still wished for her to be warned, injured, frightened, even killed. Who and why were unknown. Surely, the people from her past must have realized by now she had never represented a threat to them in the first place. They would have to know by now that she was only a broken-down, lonely woman in search of a miracle to return her to life and end the paralyzing pain. Greg had been her miracle and he had ended up paying a high price for it.

* * *

"What can I do for you today, Nadya?" the grey-haired man behind the desk asked her as the nurse ushered her in.

"Hello, Doctor. I'm having trouble going to sleep."

"Are you drinking any coffee, tea, or cola drinks in the evenings?"

"No, Doctor. Just chamomile tea."

"When did this trouble start?"

"Recently. After I was in the second accident."

"Are you in pain?"

"No. I'm not in physical pain. All I need is something to make me sleep soundly at night, so I can function at work the next day. I've tried over-the-counter remedies but they make me drowsy the next day."

"All right. I'm going to write you a prescription." he reached for his prescription pad, "I'll give you refills for a six month period. After six months, come back and see me. We'll decide whether or not you still need them."

"Thank you, Doctor." she smiled.

"Here you are. I hope you feel better soon." he handed her the prescription.

* * *

Her white Carson Drugs paper bag in her hand, she entered the lobby of The Splendid to find an unfamiliar man at the mailboxes.

"You must be Nadya." he spoke softly.

"Yes, I'm Nadya." she smiled quizzically.

"I'm Vincent Green." he extended his hand and took hers in his, squeezing it gently, "I live across the hall from you."

"It's very nice to meet you. I'm sorry I wasn't around earlier to welcome you to The Splendid."

"That's perfectly all right. I have to admit, I have noticed your name on your mailbox before. Nadya with a "y": It's Slavic, isn't it?"

"Yes, I'm Azerbaijani."

"I've been wondering what a Nadya with a "y" would be like. The alternate spelling with an "i" is the only one I run across."

"It's just plain old me. My name evokes images of sultry Garboesque femme fatales, so everyone is disappointed to find out it's only plain old me."

"You are exactly the way I envisioned a Nadya with a "y"."

"That's very kind of you. I hear the most beautiful music coming from your apartment."

"I hope it's not too loud."

"It's not loud enough. I love jazz standards. I can never get enough."

"I'm the same way."

"Please keep playing them."

They started up the stairs together, talking like two old friends who had known each other forever.

* * *

She awakened from dreams she did not want to see come to an end...

..."Still my shy girl, aren't you?" Greg was tickling her from behind, "Shy and demure, sweet and cuddly, but a wild, passionate tiger in bed...a tiger who's been waiting to be unleashed."

"You're the only one with the key to the tiger's cage, Greg."...

She re-lived that night in her dreams. She re-lived their tender moments over and over in her fitful sleep. Dreams were her only respite. She cried in the shower, dressed in one of her three "respectable enough for work" outfits, went downstairs to Mama Rosa's for her take-out morning coffee, and walked two doors to her job at Newman and Carr Office Supplies. She felt fortunate to be in the back office instead of working with the customers. She spent her lunch breaks at the office, reading a book she kept there, nibbling on raw vegetables she brought from home. After work, she walked home and barricaded herself. There had been no word from her parents since Greg's departure. They already had her where they wanted her: Alone and vulnerable again. Her only hope of maintaining her sanity was keeping them at bay.

Their absence was short-lived. She was having a meal of grapes and unsweetened yogurt with black Earl Grey tea, listening to the gentle strains of Jack Jones singing "I Wish You Love" from Vincent's apartment. Then, it happened:

"Nadya, open this door. Your mother's not here. It's just you and me. I want to talk to you."

She froze.

"I don't like the way you've been treating your mother. I want you to apologize to her. You've been a great disappointment to us, Nadya. All you've done is cause us heartache after all the sacrifices we made for you. I'm going to take you home to see her and you are going to apologize to her for what you've been putting her through. Open this door. I want to talk to you privately. You know I can get George to let me in."

She ran into the bedroom and climbed out to the fire escape. She crawled across to Vincent's side to conceal herself from view when she passed the hallway window and fire exit. She crouched under his open window. Her father's footsteps in the hallway faded away and later returned with another set of footsteps. She saw her father's hands closing and locking her bedroom window. She trembled. Vincent's face appeared at his window, and she pressed her index finger to her lips. He reached for her hand and guided her into his apartment.

"Thank you." she whispered.

"You look terrified."

"My dad just locked me out of my apartment."

"Wait here. I'll take care of this." he opened his door to see Nadya's apartment wide open and George pacing in the hallway.

"What's going on, George?"

"Her father's in there."

"George, I don't think it's proper to allow access to the lady's apartment."

"He's her dad."

"That does not give him the right to violate her privacy. She pays the rent and she decides who has access to her apartment and who doesn't. The lady does not want her parents to have access."

"This guy's got clout. He threatened to have me fired if I didn't do what he said."

"Don't worry about that. I'll talk to Sarge and make sure your job is safe."

"Sure thing, Mr. Green."

"You can leave now, George."

"Yes sir."

Vincent entered Nadya's apartment to find Boris rifling through her dresser drawers.

"Sir, you need to leave now."

"Who are you?"

"I'm Vincent Green. Nadya has not given her permission for you to be here."

"She is my daughter. I can do whatever I want."

"No sir, you can't."

"What are you, another cop?" he smirked.

"As a matter of fact, I'm a former Toronto P.D. detective."

"I should've known." he laughed; the sight of his open mouth sickened Vincent.

"Sir, you need to leave now."

"Are you sleeping with her, too? No, don't tell me. Of course you are. She must be sleeping with the entire Elmdale police force. Do yourself a favor: Don't get swept up in her drama. She loves to fabricate stories."

"She has not told me any stories."

"My daughter is a dangerous woman. She is selfish and manipulative. Don't let her make a fool of you. Nadya is a very beautiful woman, and she uses her beauty to seduce men."

"Sir, if you do not vacate these premises, I will call the police."

"You are going to be sorry you interfered in my family's business." he stormed out.

Vincent returned to his apartment.

"I'll go in with you to make sure everything's in order." he took her hand and led her back.

Her apartment felt contaminated to her now. She glanced around the living room and kitchen, however found nothing amiss. In the bedroom, she was taken aback immediately.

"I had a framed photo of Greg right here on my dresser. It's gone."

She opened a dresser drawer and searched frantically.

"My locket's gone, too. I kept it in this drawer under my scarves. The clasp on it was broken and I couldn't afford to get it fixed, so I kept it hidden...I had Greg's picture in it. My dad removed every trace of Greg..." She fell on the floor.

"Do you want to file a police report? He removed your property without your consent."

"That would only make him angrier and he'd do something worse to retaliate."

"You can't live in constant fear like this."

"You don't know what he's capable of – what both my parents are capable of. You're not safe, either. Anyone who is nice to me becomes the victim of their wrath. Look what they did to Greg. Please don't put yourself in danger."

"I am not afraid of them. Your parents have been playing games with your mind all your life."

"I heard a few snippets when you were talking to him. What he said is not true. I don't seduce men."

"I know that."

"In fact, men don't find me attractive at all."

"Obviously, Greg found you very attractive."

"Greg is my only reason for living. Thank you, Vincent...for everything. For the talk, for not letting my dad near me."

"I could tell you were afraid of him."

"I'd rather die than be alone with him."

"I won't let him hurt you, Nadya. You're safe. He can never hurt you again."

Chapter 11/ Dark River

The lights from Devon shimmered on the dark river. The distant sounds of cars and motorcycles on Queen Street echoed in the stillness. The stars dotted the dark sky. She knew well that even the most scorching afternoons ended in chilly evenings in Elmdale. Buttoning her white Banlon cardigan, she folded her arms across her chest. Melancholy music wafted through the open window on her left. It was the new neighbor's bedroom window. She had not been able to summon up the courage to initiate a conversation with the elusive, handsome man whose apartment shared a wall with her own. There already seemed to be an inevitable intimacy of hearing each other's toilets flush, showers run, snippets of phone conversations, radios, televisions and phonographs; and inhaling each other's cooking aromas. Apartment buildings afforded no degree of discretion, personal dignity, or modesty. But this was her reality now.

The heavy fire door behind her was opened and a murmur was heard.

"Lovely evening."

"It certainly is." she turned around to face the tall figure.

"May I join you?"

"You don't need to ask." she smiled.

He joined her by the railing.

"Your music is beautiful."

"I'm sorry I play it into the wee hours of the morning. I'll need to watch that."

"Please don't stop playing. It's most uplifting to be lulled to sleep by your music. Our shared wall is a blessing."

"Thank you. That's very gracious of you, Miss Field."

"Joyce, please."

"I'm Vincent."

"Both of us are embarking on this perilous journey of career change when most of our colleagues are thinking about retirement."

"We're gluttons for punishment." he smiled, "Sometimes it takes decades of doing other things to lead us to our heart's desire."

"Very true. After being up close and personal with criminals, you need to stand back and understand the inner workings of their minds. You would make a valuable consultant for the police forces around the province and a compassionate mentor for the detectives who are where you were once. You have a kind demeanor and an analytical mind."

"I can tell Sandi's been busy talking about me."

Both laughed uncomfortably.

"What about you? What made you decide to pursue Psychology?"

"I'd always been fascinated by it, but circumstances had never allowed me to pursue it. Women did not have many opportunities back then. I became a teacher, got married right out of Teacher's College, and taught music in elementary schools for twenty years. When my marriage dissolved after twenty years, I realized time was running out and I had to grab on to my dreams before it was too late."

"And now, here we both are...Do you think you might enjoy teaching at the university?"

"If I am fortunate enough to have that opportunity, yes. What about you?"

"Likewise."

"Law School seems to be a natural fit for Sandi."

"It is. I'm very happy for her." he said, "Are you cold? I can get you a blanket."

"No, please don't go to any bother."

"No bother. If you'd like, we can go inside and I can make us a hot drink."

"That would be lovely."

"I promise not to talk shop." he held the fire door open for her and opened his apartment door with the key he produced from his pocket, “You can never be too careful. Even in a small town like Elmdale.”

“I agree. I always lock up, too. I’ve got my key in my dress pocket. Elmdale is not as safe as it appears.”

“Make yourself at home.” he stood aside.

The hallway light was on. She entered the lemon-scented apartment and he followed her. His furniture was solid and rugged. Tasteful and high quality. Chocolate brown upholstery and sturdy oak tables with clean lines. Precisely the way she had envisioned his space.

“Tea all right?”

“Yes, please.”

“Please feel free to browse through my record rack and select anything you’d like to listen to at home.” he went into the adjoining kitchen with the mint green painted birch cabinets, “If you like, you can give me a list of your favorite songs once you’ve listened to them, and I’ll make you a tape.”

“That’s very kind of you, but...I don’t have a tape recorder...I mean I had one...a stereo console with a reel to reel tape recorder...but after the divorce, my ex-husband took what he wanted, and kept the house to live in with his new paramour. I moved into an apartment, so my brother offered to allow me to store my piano and stereo console at his house. I only have a portable phonograph.”

“Someday, you’ll own a whole new house and you’ll have all your belongings with you.”

“I hope so.” she deftly checked the labels of the albums in his brass record rack.

He brought two white restaurant style cup and saucer sets filled with fragrant steeped tea and returned to the kitchen for the cream and sugar.

“Thank you.” she carefully poured cream into her tea and stirred it.

"I am going to venture a guess that Sarah Vaughan's album is the first one that caught your attention." he sat on the wing chair.

"Am I that transparent?" she blushed.

"No. You are that delightful. A gentle, classy lady would enjoy listening to Sarah Vaughan."

"Flattery will get you everywhere." she laughed softly.

"I'm sorry."

"It's quite all right." her reassuring smile soothed his discomfort.

"Do you have children?" he asked.

"No. We were never blessed with children." she smiled wistfully, "What about you? Were you married? Do you have children?"

"Never married; no children."

"As a detective, it must've been difficult to meet people not connected to your work."

"I'm happy to leave it all behind...Would you like me to call Mama Rosa's and order up a couple of desserts to go with our tea?"

"Don't go to any trouble."

"No trouble. What do you like?"

"It doesn't matter. I'll go with what you like."

"Their cherry squares are delicious. Is that all right?"

"Of course."

He went into the kitchen to use the telephone. She leaned back and closed her eyes. All was well with the world again.

Chapter 12/ Hunters

The two women sat in the orange sports car parked behind Splendid Hotel. The younger one behind the steering wheel was analyzing a photograph.

"This Greg Logan is a yummy morsel. I think I'm going to enjoy this more than any of my other projects." she licked her lips and tossed back her long black hair, "Ana, how did your daughter manage to get in his pants?"

"She must've thrown herself at him when he was hopelessly drunk."

"Why would he go back to her?"

"Because she's easy."

"It still baffles me. He could have any woman he wants. Why her? I knew her back in university, and she was an outcast. All the young men laughed about her. Not much has changed in eighteen years. People still think she's a joke."

"She was only a convenience for him, I'm sure."

"What are we going to do about the new man Boris found there last week?"

"We'll have to deal with him next. Patsita, you're sure you can pull this off?"

"Ana, stop worrying. I've never met a man or a woman I couldn't seduce." She winked, "Looks like a trip to Hub City's on the horizon. Want to come along?"

"Count me in. Boris can fend for himself for a few days."

"Now, let's get today's job done before any tenants get home."

They stepped out of the car. The younger woman twisted her waist-length black hair into a knot and led the way to the fire escape. With the agility of a spider, she wove her way up the two flights of wooden stairs. Her sinuous, compact body swayed alluringly in a clingy robin blue halter top and tight denim shorts. Her fringed tan leather shoulder bag swung rhythmically on her hip. Behind her, Ana was plodding along in her orange and yellow plaid polyester pants and yellow polyester blouse. Her white shoulder bag hung awkwardly on her side. She was huffing and puffing by the time she reached Nadya's window.

"Are you sure you can get this window open, Patsy?"

"There isn't a window Patricia Gonzales cannot open. These double hung windows in older buildings are a breeze." she pried the window open effortlessly, "There, see?" she pulled it up all the way and slid in.

Ana cautiously straddled the window sill. With Patsy's help, she managed to land inside the bedroom. They proceeded to open all of the dresser drawers. Patsy pulled out an aquamarine scarf.

"What do you think?" she tied it as a turban and continued rummaging.

Ana pulled out sketch books with pencil still life drawings, and notebooks with poetry and short stories.

"Ana, you can submit her poetry as your own and have the writing career you've always wanted. She is really quite good. The campus newspaper and the yearbooks always published her work, even though she didn't know a soul at either place to vouch for her. I want the sketches, though."

"Here, take, Patsita."

"Find anything I can use for the voodoo, Ana?"

Ana held up a shiny navy blue bra with two thin, flat polyester triangles.

"Look how small."

"Looks like a training bra. She was flat as a board in university. Looks like they haven't grown since then. Did they just not develop?"

"Oh, they developed. When she was nine, she went through full-blown puberty, with 36 B cups. Just the sight of her was so repulsive to me. I couldn't even look at her after that."

"How did they get small?"

"She started binding them really tight when she turned fourteen. They eventually melted away."

"She can actually wear these teeny weeny Dici bras."

"Here, take. Use it for the voodoo. I'll get you more." she pulled out a dark brown one, a ruby one, and an emerald green one, and handed them to Patsy, "You can use them in all the spells."

"I wish we could find something belonging to Greg."

"Let me see...There is a white singlet in the bra drawer. It might be his." Ana pulled it out and smelled it, "Smells like a man. Has to be his. Must be keeping it as a souvenir."

Patsy stuffed the sketchbooks, notebooks, bras, and Greg's singlet into her bag while Ana tried on Nadya's Lucite bangles and kept them on her wrist.

"I think we're done here, Ana. We'd better get going." Patsy climbed out and took Ana's hands to ease her out.

She shut the window and walked toward the stairs when Vincent's window caught her eye.

"Didn't Boris say the new guy lived across the hall? This must be his window."

"Patsy, you're not thinking..."

"Why not?" she smiled demonically and handed her bag to Ana, "Just stay out here, Ana. Let me know if you see anyone coming."

"Be quick, Patsy."

"Don't worry." she pried his window open and climbed in, "His bedroom is impeccable."

She glanced around the room and spotted a photograph in a silver frame on top of a chest of drawers. There were three people in dark suits: A trim, grey-haired man with his arm around the shoulder of the petite woman with natural sandy blonde hair in the center, and a younger tall man with soft features and dark eyes on her other side. She took it to the window to show Ana.

"This one must be him." she pointed to the tall younger man, "Isn't he delicious? I want to get in his pants so bad!"

"What a fine example of manhood...He's the best looking man I've ever seen." Ana sighed.

Patsy returned the photo to its place and climbed out.

"I'd better take a valium when we get to the restaurant, Patsy." Ana said, "That man's picture gave me palpitations."

"Better give me one, too, Ana."

They climbed down the fire escape and returned to the car.

* * *

Mel came up the stairs to find Nadya waiting outside her apartment.

"The guys are on their way over to take fingerprints." he said," You did the right thing, not touching anything and calling me right away. The fingerprints we find may not be on file if they're amateurs or just haven't been caught before."

Olivia opened her door and glanced quizzically at them.

"Someone or some people broke into my apartment, Olivia." Nadya told her, "They came in through the bedroom window."

Olivia placed a reassuring arm around her.

"These old buildings have windows that even a child can tamper with." Mel said.

Sandra's door was opened.

"I thought I heard something about a burglary."

"Nadya's been broken into." Olivia explained, "They came in through the back window when she was at work."

"I'm very sorry to hear that."

"What did they take?" Olivia asked.

"My poetry, sketches, my favorite scarf, some bracelets, some undergarments, and Greg's undershirt."

"That is a very bizarre combination." Sandra observed, "I don't think it was a random hit by teenagers in search of drug money. It was very personal. Can you think of anyone who might want to do this to you, Nadya?"

"No. I wish I could."

"Maybe it's one of Greg's ex-girlfriends." Olivia said.

"I know all of them." Mel said, "All parted amicably."

Uniformed officers were coming up the stairs, followed by Vincent, returning from the university.

"Vince, just the man I'm looking for!" Mel said.

"What's up, Mel?"

"Can you check your apartment for signs of a break-in?"

"No problem. What's happened?"

"Nadya's been broken into." Sandra told him.

"They gained entry through the bedroom window." Mel told him, "We want to know if hers was the only apartment they hit, or if there were others that open up to the fire escape. Steve's is all right and Myrtle's old place is still empty."

"I'll check right now." Vincent entered his apartment and returned shortly, "I noticed a photograph has been moved." he said, "Sandi, it's the one of you, me, and Sgt. Sheridan."

"That's odd." she said.

"Nadya, do you have anything with only your parents' fingerprints on them?" Mel asked.

"You think they did this?"

"We're looking at all possibilities."

"I can't see my dad climbing up the fire escape."

"Perhaps someone else gained access that way and let him or both your parents in through the door."

"Nadya, Mel needs to know about last week." Vincent said.

"What happened last week?" Olivia appeared frightened.

"My dad got George to let him in and he stole a framed photo of Greg and the heart-shaped gold locket Greg gave me."

"Was there a diary stolen?" Sandi asked.

"I don't keep one."

"Smart girl." Sandi said, "They always fall into the wrong hands."

"Do you know of any younger people they associate with, who might have been helping them?" Mel asked.

"My mother has a lot of younger friends. They're into some strange things...like the occult, avant-garde art, porn..."

"Whoa!" Sandi gasped.

"I grew up in a crazy, decadent, depraved world with self-indulgent parents who preached fundamentalist religion to me and subjected me to bizarre forms of punishment for every normal, harmless thing I did. I wouldn't put anything past them or their friends."

"They sound like sick puppies." Sandi shook her head.

"I just thought of something that might have Dad's fingerprints on it." Nadya said, "He brought over a ceramic toothpick holder with his toothpicks in it, so he could pick his teeth after he had some biscuits. I've never touched it."

"Excellent." Mel said, "I'll tell the guys."

"Wait! Mom likes to snoop through my closet and criticize my taste in clothes. Her fingerprints should be on the two frilly dresses I have, one green, one purple. I've never worn them, but I did wash them before I hung them up, so there shouldn't be any fingerprints except mine and hers."

"Good." Mel returned to her apartment.

Olivia and Sandra both hugged Nadya.

"Mel, we'll all be at my place if you need Nadya." Olivia called out to him through Nadya's open door.

"Thanks, Liv." he called back.

* * *

"We found both of your parents' fingerprints in your bedroom, around the dresser area, and the window sill, along with another set of fingerprints, which were a match to the ones found on Vince's window sill and photograph." Mel told her, "We also found one long, black hair in your bedroom. We believe the hair came from the same person who left the third set of fingerprints, unless you can think of someone who was there legitimately and left the hair."

"There shouldn't be any hairs there, except mine and Greg's."

"Do you have any idea who this might be?"

"I would have to say, if I had to venture a guess, it would be one of my mother's young, bohemian friends. And, I'm afraid I have no idea where or how they can be located."

"If you think of any names or places associated with these people, call us."

"I will."

"We'll get to the bottom of this. We're making progress. It'll all be over soon." Mel reassured her.

Chapter 13/ Innocence

Laughter was emanating from the lobby. When she opened the door, the smooching couple huddled in the corner pulled apart and shot mocking glances at her.

"Hello, Nadine." the barrel-shaped blonde in the teal hot pants and hot pink bubble blouse called out, emphasizing the erroneous name.

The stench of the woman's heavy perfume co-mingling with her beau's Old Spice aftershave filled the stuffy lobby, overpowering the ever-present smell of decay.

"Such a shame you couldn't hang on to Greg." the woman called out after her as she started up the stairs, "I knew he'd grow tired of you."

Nadya did not go up to her own apartment. She knocked on my door, instead.

"Is this a bad time, Mrs. Carleton?"

"No, no. It's always a good time for you, Nadya, dear."

She tentatively stepped inside.

"Sit down, dear. I heard some commotion from the lobby. Did someone say something to upset you, dear?"

"It's not important."

"There must have been people downstairs who don't belong in the building. I'm going to mention to Sarge that we ought to have a security door like the ones they have in all the new apartment buildings. Anybody off the street can wander in here at all hours."

"These two would've found a way to get in, even if we had a security door, Mrs. Carleton."

"Who were they, dear?"

"It's a most peculiar pairing. One was Gwen, the woman who's been fixated on Greg. The other one was one of the men I saw in the lobby before – the older of the two. At that time, Greg found out he was Bok Heller, the shady businessman who's been buying all the buildings around here. They looked pretty cozy."

"That is, indeed, a peculiar pairing."

"I have a bad feeling about this, Mrs. Carleton. I can't put my finger on it, but there's something going on behind the scenes."

"I agree. Bok Heller doesn't strike me as a man who takes 'no' for an answer. I reckon he's hot under the collar because Sarge refuses to budge."

"I wonder what he's up to."

"Whatever he's up to, he's not going to succeed. We're going to continue living here just as we always have, all of us. Soon, Greg will be back and you'll feel a lot safer."

"Mrs. Carleton, Greg may not want to return to me...And, I can't blame him. All I've done is drag him down. He's suspended because of my parents' schemes. I told him before he left for Hub City that he should forget me...no visits, no phone calls...complete distance from me...If he wants to end our relationship and move on, I won't stand in his way. He deserves so much better than me, Mrs. Carleton."

"Don't you dare speak that way, Nadya! Greg is the luckiest young man to have someone like you to love him and he knows that. He'd never find another you. He's coming back to you, to build a future with you."

"You always know how to make me feel better, Mrs. Carleton. Thank you." she hugged me.

She felt so fragile in my arms, like a shivering sparrow. I held onto her a little longer and a little tighter.

None of us could deny that something sinister was brewing, and unbeknownst to us, it would sweep all of us away into oblivion.

* * *

The cool night air wrapped itself around her like a lover's embrace. She could hear "Rodrigo's Concerto" from Vincent's apartment. The fire door behind her opened and Vincent appeared, struggling with an enormous wicker picnic basket. She held the door open for him.

"What's all this?" she asked playfully.

"I heard you out here and I thought we could have a moonlight picnic." he put down the basket.

"That's so thoughtful of you, Vincent. How did you have time to prepare it? I haven't been out here that long."

"I prepared some of it in advance, in anticipation of meeting you here." he looked away from her.

"Thank you. This is a wonderful surprise."

He placed the two cable spools from each end of the fire escape together. From the basket, he produced a green gingham tablecloth, folded it in two, and spread it across the makeshift table. More surprises sprang out of the basket: A bottle of red wine, whose label she could not make out in the dim light, two wine goblets, a package of Carr's Water Crackers, two paper plates, paper napkins, and three plastic Tupperware containers of cheese cubes and grapes.

"I'm afraid I have no dessert." he said.

"Don't worry: I have dessert covered." she smiled mischievously, "I made cherry squares. I was planning to bring them over to you later."

"You're full of surprises, Joyce Field."

"So are you, Vincent Green."

He placed two of the lawn chairs in permanent use on the fire escape close together and held hers for her. They ate in silence, exchanging furtive glances and timid smiles.

"I don't think I've ever enjoyed myself this much." she said.

"Neither have I."

"Now, time for dessert." she rose and gently placed a hand on his shoulder to prevent him from getting up, "Sit back and let me wait on you for a change."

They fed each other forkfuls of the decadent cheesecake cut into squares.

The haunting melody of "Greenfields" filled the air.

"Would you like to dance?" he murmured.

"I would love to." she said, "This is the most beautiful song I've ever heard."

"It's the most beautiful song ever written." he placed a tentative arm around her as though afraid she might balk, "I knew it was next. I know the order of the songs on the tape."

She kept her own touch light, in fear of appearing clingy. He smelled of Ivory Soap, Breck Shampoo and a fresh, green deodorant. His heart was beating against her chest. She feared the beating of her own heart so near might give her away.

Anticipating the ever-familiar concluding strains of the song, he let his arms drop to his sides, like a young schoolboy at a dance recital. They stood facing each other, afraid to look directly in the other's eyes. "Yesterday When I Was Young" in Shirley Bassey's rich voice stabbed at her heart. She wondered how their lives would have turned out had they met when they were younger. She wished she were that innocent twenty-year-old she once had been, fresh out of college...She wished that her younger self had met Vincent as a baby-faced rookie officer. She wished no one else had existed for either one of them before this...They could have been the lovers in green fields.

"Joyce, are you all right?" he asked, noting the pained look on her face.

"I'm perfectly all right." she smiled and reassured him, "Listening to Shirley Bassey can be so heart-wrenching. She made me reflect on some past choices and wonder what I could've done differently."

"The past is a minefield best kept at arm's length. The bad choices from our youth made it possible for us to appreciate the right ones we're making in the present."

"You're absolutely right. Our mistakes shaped us into who we are today."

"Don't regret anything, Joyce. All that matters is: We survived and here we are...Sharing wine and cheese, cherry squares and music on the fire escape." he gazed at her with tenderness, "I don't know that I'd be here now, enjoying this lovely evening with a beautiful lady like you, if I had not taken so many wrong turns in the past."

Tony Bennett was singing "I've Grown Accustomed To Her Face". He took both her hands and pulled her close for another dance. This time, his touch was less tentative, more deliberate. When the song changed to Anne Shelton singing "Tenderly", he leaned in to kiss her – at first hesitant, unsure – then, urgent. She was afraid to open her eyes – afraid that when she did, he might vanish. When he released her, he could not meet her gaze.

"I hope I wasn't too forward."

"No, you weren't. I was hoping you'd do that."

"I've wanted to do it since the first time we spoke to one another. Your smile captivated me."

"I remember that day."

"We passed each other on the stairs, you smiled and welcomed me to The Splendid. After that day, I tried to cross paths with you again...I tried to figure out your schedule...All to no avail. I thought I was doomed to admire you from afar forever."

"Look at us now."

"You are so exquisite." he lowered his eyes.

She caressed his smooth, full cheek. With an unexpected urgency, he pulled her to himself. She did not want him to let go. His arms felt so right. They felt like home.

"I'd better take you home." he released her.

"Let's gather up our picnic things first." she said, placing the empty Tupperware containers, empty wine glasses and the tablecloth back in the basket, and gathering the paper plates, used napkins and the packaging from the crackers in a pile.

"I'll get a trash bag for those once we get everything else inside." he said, taking the basket from her.

She refused to allow him to carry her Pyrex baking dish and the two forks. He placed the basket in front of his apartment door and took the dish from her, so she could unlock her door. She turned on her hallway light and took them into her kitchen. She returned to bid him good night.

"Thank you for sharing this evening with me, Joyce."

"Thank you for inviting me. I had a wonderful time, Vincent."

He kissed her again – less tentative this time.

"Good night, Joyce. Can I see you tomorrow?"

"I'd love that. Good night, Vincent."

She closed her door and leaned against it, tears streaming down her cheeks.

Chapter 14/ Last Days Of Summer

Summers in Elmdale were hot, intense, and short. Apartment dwellers sought relief on fire escapes and rooftops. Balconies and air conditioners were few and far between back then. Elmdale was behind the times in welcoming modern trends. We barely noticed what we lacked. No one complained. People made do with what they had.

None of us knew the history of The Splendid. We wondered when it was built, whether it had ever been a hotel, and what the original façade had been. No one was able to provide us with answers. The blue mosaic tile façade had to have been a mid-century embellishment. So few buildings in town had this attractive feature, and the ones that did were mid-century buildings which had replaced burnt Victorian ones. Older buildings like our Splendid were either brick or clapboard. This dichotomy deepened the mystery and endeared our home to us even more.

Summer was nearing its end. Remaining days on the fire escape were in short supply. The kids spent as much time there as they could steal from their active lives.

On that Sunday afternoon, Mel's portable turntable was perched on a cable spool. Gentle strains of Simon and Garfunkel's "Bridge Over Troubled Water" lingered in the humid air. Mel took a swig from a stubby beer bottle. In her tangerine halter dress, Gayle sat beside him.

"Hey, is this a private party, or can anybody join?" a jovial voice was heard from the second floor window directly below Vincent's.

"Come on out, Steve." Mel said, "There's plenty of cold beer."

The young man climbed out and took one of the empty chairs.

"This is the life, man. You've got a great view of the river here." he took the beer Mel offered him.

"I love this place." Gayle said.

"There are some very interesting people living here."

"Ahem...We know who you mean." Mel smirked, "Take a cold shower, man. She's way out of your league."

"She's a knockout."

"She only dates distinguished older gentlemen. She's got no time for kids."

"Olivia wouldn't give you the time of day." Gayle laughed, "I've got to start supper." she rose from her chair.

"What're we having?"

"Chili."

"Can I come over?" Steve pleaded.

"Yes, son." Mel patted him on the head.

"See you guys in a while." Gayle went in through the fire exit.

Upstairs, unnoticed by the others, Nadya was leaning against the railing. Living without Greg was something she was not strong enough to do. From Vincent's window, Jack Jones, the misty-eyed crooner could be heard singing "I Wish You Love". Why should Greg be stuck with a lame duck like her? She knew she was living on borrowed time. When he was no longer happy, she would let him go. She would never beg him to stay. Women like her always ended up alone. She had no illusions. Loving someone meant wanting what was best for them. She had never been anyone's idea of best.

* * *

"How are you doing, Nadya, dear?" I hugged her.

"I'm okay, Mrs. Carleton."

"I was just fixing myself a snack, dear: Cheez-Whiz on white bread. Would you like some?"

"Yes, thank you. Let me help you make them."

"It's all made and there's enough to feed an army." I carried my platter of oozing triangles into the living room and placed it on the coffee table.

"I'll make the tea." Nadya was familiar with our routine.

"Are you up for watching some 'Cannon'?" I asked her.

Her face lit up. Police dramas were her elixir. The times we watched them together were the only times I saw her animated.

"You really miss Robert T. Ironside, don't you?" I said.

"I miss him terribly. It's so unfair that all we can get are Calais affiliate channels for all the American networks. They stop showing so many series that are still being shown by other affiliates."

"I miss him, too. I'm hoping one of our channels will pick up reruns of Perry Mason, so you can see your 'Perfect Dad' again."

"If he were my dad, he wouldn't clip my wings. He would teach me to fly and never give up my dreams. I hope I get to be Raymond Burr's daughter in heaven."

"I hope you do, too, Nadya. I think Raymond Burr would be right proud to be your dad."

"When I get to heaven, I'll be the person I was meant to become, not the one I ended up becoming."

* * *

Arlene was fumbling in her purse looking for her mailbox key. The pudgy younger woman beside her hit her arm.

"Who is that dreamboat coming down the stairs?"

"I have no idea, Kristy." Arlene said without looking up.

"Look over there."

"Hello, ladies." Steve brushed past them with a smirk and winked at Kristy on his way out.

"Sounds like Steve, the one subletting Greg's apartment." Arlene opened her mailbox and gathered her bills.

"He winked at me!"

"I'm happy for you, Kristy. For Pete's Sake, is this what they teach you at that university?"

"I want to get an apartment in your building. You and I can hang out all the time, Cous."

"Forget it. Every man in the building would need a bodyguard if you were set loose around here."

"Come on, Cous. Put in a good word for me with the landlord."

"You only come to visit me so you can check out all the men who live here."

"Arlene!" Kristy dug her nails into her arm, "Oh my God!"

"What is it now?"

"Someone's coming in the front door...What a gorgeous hunk of a man."

"Kristy, cut this out right now!"

"Hello, Arlene." Vincent greeted her.

"Hello, Vince."

"It's nice out, isn't it?"

"Sure is. Vince, this is my little cousin, Kristy Simmons. She's a sophomore at the university."

"Nice to meet you." he smiled.

"Nice to..." she was gaping slack-jawed at the object of her lust.

The front door was opened again and Nadya entered in her blue trench coat. She greeted Arlene, retrieved her mail and started up the stairs with Vincent.

"Did you see that?" Kristy was fuming, "That man-eating bitch gets all the cute guys! First, she took that sexy Greg away from me."

"Greg was never yours to be taken away."

"Now, she's got her hooks into this dreamboat. That slut! I'm not going to let her steal Steve from me, too. I'm going to stake my claim."

"I'm sure she won't mind that one little bit." Arlene shook her head in exasperation and started toward the stairs.

* * *

"Greg's coming back." Mel announced, "When he heard about the break-in, he went ballistic. I tried to keep that from him but one of the guys accidentally leaked it."

"What about me?" Steve leapt to his feet, "Where am I going to live?"

"Slow down, cowboy. You're going to stay where you are. He's moving in with Nadya."

"How's all his stuff going to fit in there?" Steve asked.

"He's only going to take what he really needs and leave the rest in storage." Gayle explained.

"Myrtle would've had a field day with this if she were still living here." Sandra laughed.

Mama Rosa approached their table with a bottle of champagne and patted Vincent on the head.

"Vinnie, my boy, the lady at that table back there sent you this bottle of champagne and this card."

"Can you take them back, please, Mama Rosa?" he lowered his eyes and fidgeted with his napkin.

"No use letting expensive booze go to waste." Steve said, "We can share it. Open the card, Vince."

"No, I don't want any of it."

"I'll open it, then." Steve reached across the table and ripped the envelope open, "The old doll hasn't taken her eyes off you since you got here, Vince."

"She's one of his professors." Sandra said, "She's been coming on really strong lately."

"'Room #236, Lord Chilton Hotel, 8 p.m.'" Steve read the card aloud.

Vincent buried his face in his hands. Steve cast a knowing glance at the woman and winked at her.

"I'll go in your place. I've never fucked a professor before." he snickered.

The woman rose from her table and crossed the restaurant to where Steve was seated. She poured his beer over his head before storming out.

"You were asking for it!" Mel said, roaring with laughter.

Nadya and Olivia entered the restaurant to find everyone except Vincent and Joyce laughing.

"What did we miss?" Olivia asked.

"You won't believe it when you hear it." Gayle said.

"Why are you soaking wet?" Olivia asked Steve.

"He hit on the wrong woman." Mel explained.

"Is that why you're all laughing?" Olivia wanted to know.

"No. There's plenty more." Gayle told her.

"Vincent just had a close call." Sandra explained, "His amorous professor sent him this bottle of champagne and a card with a room number on it."

"You should've seen her, too." Gayle continued, "Get a load of this: A burgundy wool hat with a veil and an ostrich feather, teal eye shadow, scarlet lipstick, jet black hair tied back in a chignon, slinky dress with cleavage, six inch heels..."

Olivia's eyes widened in astonishment.

"What's a chignon?" Steve asked.

"A ballerina style bun." Arlene explained.

"It would look far-out on you, Olivia." Steve placed his hand on her knee.

She slapped his hand and shot back a glance at him that turned him pale.

Across the table, Vincent nudged Joyce subtly and the two of them rose, excused themselves and walked out of the restaurant.

Chapter 15/ Insurance

"You want cooking tips from me?" Sandra's laughter rang out throughout Mama Rosa's and attracted the attention of the other patrons, "You must be really desperate if you're asking me!"

"You know your way around a kitchen far better than I do, Sandi. Any help you can give me would be greatly appreciated."

"Aha. You're trying to impress a certain pretty lady, aren't you? You sly dog." she poked him in the ribs.

Beet red, he glanced around the restaurant. Customers at nearby tables snickered.

"I've been watching you. I've noticed you gazing longingly in a particular lady's direction and exchanging shy smiles with her."

"I didn't realize we were that obvious."

"Remember, I share a wall with her. I can hear the two of you when you're over there...Don't worry: I only share a wall with her kitchen – not her bedroom." she winked.

"What kind of an animal do you think I am?" he lowered his voice almost to a whisper, "I would never pressure her into taking our relationship to that level. She's a demure, classy lady. I respect her."

"I'm just kidding. I know that. I want you to know I'm very happy for you, Vince. You're one lucky guy. She's a very special lady. Don't let her get away."

"I hope I don't do anything to mess it up."

"I think Joyce is a very understanding woman. I can't see her walking away that easily. I can finally say you've met the caliber of woman I always hoped you would."

"Thank you. This feels so different. Unfamiliar territory. I didn't think I could feel this way about anyone."

“You are both extremely sensitive souls, and easily exploited by unscrupulous people – like all your former lady friends and her ex-husband. It makes my heart happy to see the two of you together.”

“Thank you, Sandi. That means a lot to me.”

“Now, back to your cooking dilemma: Have you cooked for her before?”

“I’ve either ordered from here or taken her out to other restaurants. She’s been very generous and gracious in sharing her culinary creations with me.”

“That’s the kind of person she is – gracious, generous, kind...I can’t think of a single fault that woman has.”

“She’s remarkable. I don’t know how I lived before I met her. I hope she won’t be disappointed in me.”

“She won’t.” she patted him on the shoulder, “Not until she tastes your cooking.”

“I don’t know what to prepare for her. She’s such a superb cook; she prepares roast beef dinners, roast chicken dinners, complete with roasted vegetables. Her rice dishes are like nothing I’ve ever tasted before. And she makes it look so effortless.”

“Tell you what: We’ll look through my pathetic collection of recipes and see if we can find something suitable. Don’t worry. No matter what you prepare for her, and how it turns out, she’ll be happy that you took the time to cook for her. And that is the only thing that matters, my friend.”

* * *

She studied the lone piece of mail she retrieved from her mailbox.

“Everything okay?” Olivia, who was locking her mailbox, glanced at her.

“It’s all right, Liv.” she showed her the small envelope, “Just a craft magazine soliciting business. I subscribed to it many years ago.”

Olivia observed the typed business envelope and noticed it was addressed to Joyce Chambers. 289 King's College Road was crossed out and 303 Queen Street, Apartment 10 was scrawled under it.

"I haven't been Joyce Chambers for over five years. I changed my name back to my maiden name after the divorce." she crumpled it and enclosed it in her fist, "I don't know why Eugene would bother redirecting it to me."

"Men don't make any sense, Joyce." Olivia placed an arm around her shoulder, "Are we still on for the Poppy Family concert on Wednesday?"

"Of course we are. I'm looking forward to our 'Ladies' Night' out."

"Are we going in one or two cars?"

"Arlene has offered to take all five of us in her Parisienne. Parking might be a problem at the rink."

"We can go out for drinks afterwards." Olivia said, "I'm meeting up with Paul at Mama Rosa's after I get changed tonight. We're going to a movie after dinner. I hope he hasn't picked another action thriller."

"I hope you have a wonderful evening."

"Thank you."

As they started up the stairs, they could hear Arlene playing Dolly Parton on her stereo.

"See you later, Joyce." Olivia placed her briefcase on the floor and unlocked her door.

"Enjoy your evening, Liv."

Hearing their voices, Arlene turned down the volume on her stereo. Joyce felt a twinge. She wished she could knock on Arlene's door and tell her she did not need to worry about disturbing the neighbors by playing her music at moderate volume. If anyone was so uptight that they objected to this considerate woman's choice or volume of music, Arlene could send them to her. She could not think of anyone in the building who would complain. Myrtle was gone.

The only wild card was Ethel, who lived directly below Arlene. But Blanche had a calming effect on her.

She stood in her tiny foyer, undecided. In the end, she thought it best to mention it to her later when they had a moment alone on Wednesday. She stepped out of her pumps and put on her ballet slippers. She hung up her coat in the tiny coat closet. The crumpled envelope was promptly tossed into the bathroom wastepaper basket. In her bedroom, she removed her pale pink plaid suit with the pleated skirt and her white polyester blouse; she hung them up with meticulous care in the closet. She removed her pantyhose and left it at the foot of the bed to be hand washed later. Her black palazzo pants and fine-gauge black V-neck felt soft against her skin. Washing off her makeup, she tied her hair back partially with an elastic. In the kitchen, she removed a tall, slender green bottle of Perrier from her refrigerator and poured herself a glass of the refreshing elixir. She was lounging on her sofa, indulging in the throat-caressing delight when she heard a loud crash coming from Nadya's apartment. She bolted, unaware of the spilled drink on her sweater, placed her drink on a coaster, grabbed her keys from the coffee table, locked her door, and ran down the hall.

"Nadya, are you all right?" she called out.

"I'm sorry about the noise, Joyce." she opened the door.

"Honey, I'm not concerned about the noise. I wondered if you were hurt."

"I'm fine. I was doing some organizing in the kitchen and I dropped some things."

There were plastic containers, metal tins, and broken dishes strewn across the kitchen floor.

"Do you need some help?"

"That's okay. I'm almost done, but please come in. I'll put on some tea."

"I'll help you with this stuff on the floor." Joyce knelt down to gather the plastic containers; one of them rattled and she observed

Nadya freeze and turn pale. Her heart sank. "Nadya I don't mean to pry, but what's in this container, dear?"

"My insurance policy." Nadya mumbled.

"May I see it?"

She nodded. Joyce opened it with trepidation. Three unopened prescription bottles were nesting inside.

"Is it all right if I read the labels?" she lifted one of them.

"Yes."

"Nadya, these are heavy duty sleeping pills. It looks like you've never opened them. And there are three more refills left."

"They're my insurance policy." she lowered her eyes, "In case I end up in a situation I can't escape from any other way."

"Nadya," Joyce rose to her feet and placed the container of bottles on the kitchen table, "There's always another way...There's always hope."

"Hope is for the naïve."

"We all need hope."

"There's no hope for me. If Greg leaves me and I lose my job, I'll end up in my parents' clutches again – and that's a fate worse than death. I need to be prepared to make my escape."

"There are people who care about you, who won't let that happen. They will never get their hooks into you again – no matter what."

"No one can prevent it. They're too powerful. No one can help me."

"Nadya, it will never come to that; you'll see. Allow yourself to have hope. Your name means hope."

"How did you know?"

"Vincent's half Polish, so he's familiar with Slavic names. I asked him about your name because I've always loved it. Nadya is short for Nadezhda, and it means hope." she opened her arms to enclose her and pressed her head to her chest, "Don't give up hope, no matter what...If things ever get that bad, remember I'm always here for you. Don't forget that. Come to me. I'll find a way to get you back on your feet, so your parents can never hurt you again. Do we have a deal?"

"Joyce, you're such an amazing person. I don't know what to say."

"Say you agree to come to me if things get out of hand. You are a caring, sensitive, intelligent woman with so much to offer, so many lives yet to touch. If you end your life, your parents will have won. Don't let them have the satisfaction. Don't let them win. Fight for your life." she stood back to wipe Nadya's tears with her fingertips.

"I don't know if I'm strong enough."

"You've already survived the most horrific upbringing. You've proven how strong and capable you are."

"Thank you."

"You don't need the insurance policy anymore. You can cancel it. Why don't you let me take these?"

Nadya nodded.

"You know I'm always here for you."

"Thank you."

"I have some lemon chiffon cake at home. I'll grab it and bring it over. We can have it with our tea. Then, we can handle the organizing and cleaning up together." she took the container of pills, "I'll be right back."

Chapter 16/ Indian Summer

Autumn crept up on us like a weasel. September was deceptively dry and calm. Even the leaves were still green. Then, October arrived with overstuffed luggage in tow, mocking us with his merciless gales. He painted the city brown in wide brush strokes. Early November gifted us with a late and unexpected Indian Summer. In Elmdale, Indian Summers were like ill-fated trysts that ended abruptly. You hung on to every breathless moment, constantly looking over your shoulder.

Nadya climbed down the fire escape with an agility one would not have expected to the parking lot behind the building where a silver Celica had just parked. Greg emerged from the driver's side, ran to her and lifted her up in the air, twirling her around. They kissed like teenagers in the first flush of youth. Their arms wound around each other, they walked around the side of the building to the front door. Their laughter resonated throughout the building. They locked her apartment door behind them. He spun her around, planting soft kisses all over her face. Feverishly, she engulfed him in a steamy kiss and pulled off his T-shirt. When he took off her long peasant dress, he discovered she was wearing nothing under it. She coaxed him down to the floor on top of her. His lovemaking made her feel so intensely alive, every nerve in her body was electrified.

"I missed this." he collapsed beside her.

"So did I. Madly."

"I'm never going to be away from you again."

"I'm going to hold you to that." she propped herself on her elbow.

"All this time away from you, I was going out of my mind. I kept imagining other guys stealing you away from me."

"You know that could never happen. I'm yours and yours alone for as long as you want me, Greg."

"I'll always want you, Nadya. This is for keeps."

* * *

In the afternoons, he picked her up after work and they strolled down the street, defiantly flaunting their love. They laughed, teased each other, and kissed in wild abandon. The rest of us smiled at the sight of them, playing hide and seek with an inexplicable sense of foreboding.

* * *

I was on my way to Mama Rosa's for my decadent breakfast when I crossed paths with young Steve in uniform.

"Hey, Mrs. C." he greeted me, eyes glazed, blond hair unruly under his cap.

"Good morning, Steve. Are you all right, dear?"

"I haven't been getting much sleep lately, Mrs. C. I work days now, but it's not much better."

"Oh, dear."

"It's that new guy, Fred, who moved into Myrtle's old place across from me. He and his friend were making a lot of noise moving his stuff when I was working nights and trying to sleep days. Now that I work days, he throws loud parties that go on all night, so I still can't sleep."

"I'm so sorry, dear. Doesn't he have a job to go to?"

"He supposedly works at the shoe factory on York Street. Must be one cushy job: You never have to show up. Something's fishy about this guy. His friend's fishy, too. Iggy or something."

"Do you have time to have some breakfast with me, Steve?"

"I sure do. I'd love it, Mrs. C." he took my arm.

"A good, hearty breakfast is important for a hard-working young man."

"My mom always said that, too."

We took the window seat and a smiling young waitress approached us. Steve immediately perked up.

"What'll you have?"

"Mrs. C., you first."

"I'll have the bacon and two egg special."

"How do you like your eggs?"

"Scrambled, please."

"Coffee?"

"No, tea please. But I think this fine young officer's in need of some coffee."

"You've got that right, Mrs. C." he winked, "I'll have the Hungry Man Special with bacon, sausage, eggs and pancakes."

"How would you like your eggs, Officer?" she batted her eyelashes flirtatiously.

"Over easy." he flashed his boyish grin.

"I'll be right back with your orders."

"There she goes again." Steve pointed to a beat-up station wagon.

"Who, dear?"

"Gwen. Real head case. She circles around like a vulture."

"Is she one of the people involved in harassing Nadya?"

"Yes, but she's not connected to her parents. She's got her own delusional motives."

"Are the others gone now, Steve?"

"They're lying low. But this one's a real psycho. She's lusting after Greg and she believes in her sick mind that, if Nadya were dead, Greg would be all hers."

"Dear God, Steve!"

"Don't worry, Mrs. C. Me and the guys are on the case."

"I know she's in good hands, dear."

"We're not going to let anyone hurt Nadya."

"Bless your heart, dear."

The attractive waitress returned with our plates. Steve flashed his impeccable teeth in a seductive smile. She giggled.

"What's the story with this Gwen?" I asked.

"She's a divorcee. In her mid-fifties. A social worker. She's known to associate with some fringe types, revolutionary types, druggies and such."

"Isn't she too old for Greg?"

"Greg's totally grossed out by her. But it's not because of her age. She's done some bizarre things to other women in the past if they were in any way connected to men she was obsessed with, even if they were not romantic rivals. Gwen's a sick puppy."

"Hasn't anyone been able to do something legally?"

"She's got connections. She's untouchable. Probably sleeps with rich, influential, crooked men in high places, desperate for a blow job. Excuse my language, Mrs. C."

"That's all right. I wish someone could bring her down. She sounds like a malignant tumor. She needs to be removed before her poison spreads."

"You're right, Mrs. C. Now, watch this: She's got his routine down pat. She was circling around when he walked Nadya to work, and walked back. She's back because this is around the time he buys a newspaper from Eat-Rite and comes in here for coffee...And, there he is, off to Eat-Rite. She's driving at snail's pace, her eyes on him the whole time."

We resumed our gastronomical adventure in silence until Steve caught sight of her again.

"Now, look...He's coming back...Ooh, he's bought flowers for Nadya...Lookee here, there's Gwen right behind him."

"Doesn't she have a job to go to?"

"With her connections, she doesn't have to lift a finger."

"She's gone now."

"When he comes downstairs for his coffee, she'll start circling again, hoping for a glimpse of him through the window."

"She's coming back."

"You can set your watch by her."

Gwen came to a stop outside our window. I took a long, hard look at her. She had the appearance of a woman who might have been adequately attractive in her youth, however, had aged unattractively, due to living hard and fast. The smug grin on her face sent a chill down my spine. I had come face to face with true evil.

"Mrs. C., I'm afraid I'll have to get to work." Steve rose, "Let me treat you to this breakfast."

"No, dear, let me treat you."

"Tell you what: You let me treat you this time and I'll have a rain check from you for tomorrow."

"You've got a deal."

"Have a good day, Mrs. C. See you tomorrow."

"Same time, same place. Be careful, Steve."

He waved on his way to the cash register in search of the attractive waitress.

* * *

"What a great surprise that the pipes burst at your work and you got a holiday." Greg buried his face in her chest on the living room floor, "I just want to devour you. I can't get enough of you."

"I wish I could dissolve through your pores and live inside your heart." she stroked his glossy black hair.

A firm knock on the door startled them.

"We weren't that loud." she said, "The new tenant downstairs must be mad."

"I'll get it." he scrambled to his feet and wrapped the green crocheted afghan from the sofa around himself.

She disappeared into the bedroom and put on her long purple robe. He opened the door to a uniformed postal carrier.

"Special delivery for Na...Nay...Nad..."

"Nadya." Greg corrected the young man.

"Nadya Ba...Bay...Bab..."

"Babayevski." Greg said impatiently.

"I need a signature."

"I'll sign it."

"Are you Nadya?"

"Do I look like a Nadya to you?"

"I don't know, sir." the young man appeared puzzled.

Greg signed the sheet and the young man handed him a manila envelope, swiftly making his exit.

"Were you expecting anything in the mail?" Greg studied the envelope with a frown, "No return address."

"I wasn't expecting anything." she came into the room and tore it open.

What awaited them inside, they could never have anticipated.

Photographs of a nude Greg in a motel room surrounded by scantily-clad women slapped them on the face.

"Sweetheart, I don't know where this came from. I was never unfaithful to you. Never." he broke into tears, "I would never do that to you! I did not do this!"

"It must be superimposed. Someone did this just to hurt us." she turned to him, tears streaming down her cheeks.

"Nadya, I would never hurt you like this...I swear on my own life, I did not...would not...could not cheat on you!"

There was another knock at the door.

"It's just me." Mel called out.

A tearful Greg opened it. Mel was holding a manila envelope in his hand.

"I see you've got one, too." Greg said, "The gift that keeps on giving."

"That's not all. I got a phone call. They sent one to Fraser and one to the chief, too."

"Who's doing this?" Nadya placed her arm around Greg.

"Do you have any idea when, where and how these pictures could've been taken?" Mel asked.

"I do remember one night about six weeks ago when I was out drinking alone. After I came back from the men's room and finished my drink, everything went dark. I don't remember anything until the next day when I woke up in a motel room alone and naked. I wondered how I ended up there. I thought some of the guys I knew were playing a joke on me...found me drunk and took me there..."

"These women in the pictures...Do any of them look familiar to you?"

"No. I've never seen them before."

"They obviously drugged your drink."

"I was only gone for a few minutes."

"They must've been watching from a nearby table. Did you notice anything suspicious before you blacked out?"

"No. I wasn't looking around. I was drowning my sorrows."

"Any women try to proposition you?"

"Some. But I wasn't paying any attention. I didn't see what they looked like."

"When you came to, the next day, did you notice anything missing from your wallet?"

"No. Everything was intact. My watch and ring, too."

"This was not staged as a spur of the moment prank. It took weeks in the planning."

"Wait...Let me see this closer..." Nadya pulled out one of the photos, "This woman here: I know her."

"You do?" Greg's eyes widened.

"I do. It's Patricia Gonzales. She's a local artist and one of my mother's friends."

"Are you sure it's her?"

"I'm positive. That spider and cobweb tattoo on her upper arm is quite distinctive."

Greg kissed her cheek.

"I went to university with her. I saw that tattoo all the time during warm weather."

"This is very helpful, Nadya." Mel said, "Someone's after your badge, pal. This Patricia Gonzales and her entourage are just the flunkies. We'll get to the bottom of this."

He turned to leave, however, paused to admire Greg's afghan.

"Love the casual attire, man. The green brings out your eyes."

Once they were alone, Nadya enclosed Greg in her arms and kissed his face as he wept softly.

“They can’t tear us apart.” she murmured, “I love you and believe in you and I won’t let anyone hurt you in any way.”

Chapter 17/ Relentless

She studied him dressing for his appointment with Dr. Nicholas for his required psychological counselling. With deep longing, her eyes took in his breath-taking beauty as he shaved his smooth, youthful cheeks and put on a subtle lotion reminiscent of the ocean.

"I hope I look presentable enough." he turned to her after putting on his blue shirt and charcoal suit.

Her adoring eyes followed every line of his body.

"You're scrumptious." she stroked his cheeks and traced his soft, full lips, "You are luminous."

"I love you so much." he kissed her, "You're my anchor, my rock."

"You are mine, too. I feel so blessed to be with you, Greg."

"I'm the lucky one, Nadya." he kissed her again.

"I don't want to mess up your suit." she attempted to smooth out his tie and blazer.

"I don't care." he pulled her close, "Are you going to be all right alone, sweetie?"

"Of course I am. Don't worry about me."

"If your parents show up, call 911."

"I don't think they'll show up."

"Now that Patricia Gonzales has been charged, they might be on the rampage. They might try to pressure you into getting me to drop the charges."

"I won't let them in."

"I don't like to leave you alone when other people on this floor aren't home."

"You don't have to worry, sweetheart."

"I think Vince is coming home soon. You can crawl out to the fire escape and hide at his place, like the time you told me about."

"Everything's going to be fine. Please don't worry about me. Concentrate on your appointment." she kissed him, "I love you."

"I love you. Lock this door."

"I will."

She locked the door and turned on Greg's stereo console, which he had brought in from storage. She placed a fresh spool of tape on the reel to reel recorder and pressed the button to enable it to record directly from the turntable, without recording external interference. She put on a Ray Conniff record and sat back to savor the rich stereo sound. The loud knock on the door jolted her back to reality.

"We know you're in there, so, no use trying to evade us. We can hear your dreadful music."

She wondered if Vincent was home yet, though it was still too early. She ventured out to the fire escape through her bedroom window while the music played on and tapped on Vincent's window. He was not home. She climbed down to the lower fire escape and tapped on Steve's window. He appeared in his pajamas.

"I'm so sorry I woke you, Steve. No one else is home. My parents are at the door; they want to retaliate for Patsy getting caught. Greg told me not to let them in."

"No sweat, Nadya. I'll come right up with you. Just let me get my badge...Okay. All set." he climbed out of his window in pajamas and followed her upstairs to her window.

Her parents were still calling out from the hallway. Steve opened the door and flashed his badge.

"You'll have to leave the premises. The lady doesn't want to see you."

"Who is this? A third boyfriend? This one still has peach fuzz. Robbing the cradle now, are you?" Ana glared at him.

"I told you, she's sleeping with the entire Elmdale P.D.!"

"You were right, Boris." she turned to Nadya, "You've brought dishonor and shame upon the family and you're going to be punished!"

"Ma'am, you'll have to leave now." Steve stated firmly.

"You're going to pay for what you did to my Patsita!" Ana attempted to strike Nadya, however, Steve restrained her.

"What's going on here?" Vincent, who was returning home, stood in the doorway.

"There's the other one I told you about, Ana." Boris remarked, "She's sleeping with him, too."

"Officer Henderson and I are not romantically involved with your daughter. There is only one man in Nadya's life and they are deeply committed to each other." Vincent said.

"They're living in sin!" Ana shouted.

"They're engaged to be married."

"You're a demon child! Selfish ingrate. We're ashamed of you. You're nothing but a worthless, lazy, stupid whore! A spiteful, immoral piece of trash! You should never have been born!"

"You need to leave." Vincent stated authoritatively.

"Were you so jealous of Patsy that you wanted to hurt her like this? She's got everything going for her. She's not a failure like you. And, if you think your boyfriend is going to stick around, think again! No man could ever want you. You've got nothing to offer. He'll be tired of you in a month."

"If you do not leave, Officer Henderson will be forced to call for backup." Vincent warned them, "He has been extremely tolerant and courteous with you, but others will not be."

Muttering under her breath in Azeri, Ana took Boris' arm and led him out.

"I'm so sorry, Steve." Nadya said.

"That's okay. I have a feeling I'll be telling my grandkids about this someday."

"You're being very gracious about this. Thank you."

"No problem. Glad I could help. Take care."

"Thank you, Steve." Vincent said, "I'm glad you were here for Nadya."

"See you guys later." he climbed out to the fire escape.

"I'm sorry I wasn't home." Vincent said.

"I feel like the biggest loser running to you guys for help."

"You're in unusual circumstances. No one can deal with this stuff on their own. It's perfectly normal to ask for help, you know."

"Thank you."

"Your parents have no right to treat you this way."

"I'm used to it."

"You should never have to get used to being mistreated." he said, "Are you going to be all right?"

"Of course I am. Thank you, Vincent."

"Keep this door locked. Greg should be back soon. In the meantime you know I'm here."

"I will. Thank you."

She returned to the long-forgotten stereo. The record had long ago given up the ghost. The tape was recording dead air. She pressed "Stop" on the tape recorder and rewound it slightly in order to locate the end of the last song. She stopped to check for music, however, found only silence. She rewound it more and found the tape halfway through "Moscow Nights", the last song on the record. She listened to the remainder of it, stopped the tape, and turned off the stereo. She sat down and buried her face in her hands. When she heard Greg's key in the lock, she wiped her tears and ran to greet him. He was carrying a bouquet of pink and white roses. She flung her arms around him.

"What a warm welcome." he kissed her.

"I missed you."

"I missed you, too." he handed her the bouquet.

"Thank you, sweetheart. You are the most thoughtful man in the world. How was your appointment?"

"It went really well. He's a nice man. His private practice is in his own home. He teaches Psychology at the university. He knows Vince, Joyce and Olivia. I think this is going to be good. I'm glad you convinced me to go to a Clinical Psychologist instead of a Psychiatrist. Most people don't even know the difference."

"It's a huge difference." she arranged the roses she had placed in a green vase, "I'm going to put on supper. I meant to start it earlier, but it wasn't meant to be."

"Did they show up?"

"It's okay. They left without too much fuss."

"They still have people tracking our movements! Damn it! Those assholes knew I wouldn't be here!"

"Sweetheart, it's okay. They're gone now. Steve came up to chase them away. Then, later on, Vincent came home and provided reinforcement."

"I'm glad you're all right. Tomorrow, we're going to get our marriage licence and set up a time for a Justice Of The Peace to marry us."

"Greg..."

"We'll have a civil ceremony now, and when all the dust settles, we can have a church wedding. Is that all right?"

"It's better than all right."

"My suspension will be over in the new year, if all goes well. I hope there are no more curve balls. I dodged a bullet with that Patricia Gonzales stuff. You saved my neck when you recognized her tattoo."

"I hope we'll have a lifetime of saving each other from the bad guys."

* * *

"Blanche, they're living in sin!" Ethel plunked herself down on my sofa.

"Ethel, give those kids a break. Who cares if they are? They love each other. They're not hurting anyone. Just let it go." I put on the kettle.

"Blanche, you're turning into a hippie in your old age."

"I just have better things to do than judge people." I retorted, slamming my cupboard doors, "Those kids have been to hell and back. Leave them alone! Why can't people just let them be?"

Chapter 18/ The Offering

December washed over us with a gentle hand. On the twelfth, a month after Greg's 44th birthday, Nadya and Greg were married by a Justice Of The Peace, with Mel and Olivia as their witnesses. Back home, the rest of us were preparing a surprise reception at Mama Rosa's. Greg's family occupied the majority of the seats in the restaurant. We were the only family Nadya had. Mel and Olivia brought them back here after the ceremony. At five o'clock, it was already pitch dark. In her simple white cocktail-length dress with crocheted embellishments, Nadya appeared other-worldly. In his dark suit, Greg was the epitome of a dashing matinee idol.

I took a seat by the window at a table with Arlene, Gayle and Steve.

"They make such a gorgeous couple." Arlene was dabbing at her eyes with a tissue, "She's so beautiful. Greg's one lucky guy. They were destined to be together."

"She's going to toss the bouquet." Gayle said, "Let's go over there."

"Come on, Mrs. C." Arlene tugged at my arm.

"No, thanks, dear." I patted her hand, "That ship sailed a long time ago."

"You should've gone with them, Mrs. C." Steve said after the girls left the table.

"Not at my age, dear."

"You're a youthful, attractive lady, Mrs. C. Any older gentleman would be honored to have you at his arm."

"You're such a charmer, Steve."

"I caught it! I caught it!" Arlene returned to the table, flushed and giddy, carrying the bouquet of daisies.

"Maybe Leroy's finally going to pop the question." Steve said.

"Maybe she'll meet someone new." Gayle said, "Old Leroy's been dragging his feet for years. Maybe he's not the one for you, Arlene. You deserve to be with someone who doesn't hesitate. Someone who can't live without you."

"Right on, sister." Steve said.

"No comments from the peanut gallery." Gayle shot back at him.

"They're not doing the speeches and all that other usual stuff." Arlene said, "Greg's family knows Nadya has no blood relatives, so they wanted it to be low key."

"That's very considerate." I said, "We love her like family, but we don't have any childhood anecdotes or embarrassing stories of her teenage years."

"They're good people. They'll treat her right, Mrs. C." Gayle said.

"She deserves to be loved and appreciated. She's very special." I said.

Photographs were being taken and the kids tugged at my sleeves to get in on the activity. This blissful occasion was preserved lovingly in color to be treasured.

When I went up to congratulate them, I was overwhelmed by a sense of impending doom. Both of them felt weightless in my arms. I held Nadya close to me and kissed her forehead.

"I'll take good care of her, Mrs. C. You know that." Greg reassured me, noticing my tears.

"I know that, dear." I stroked his cheek, "I love you both."

The three of us embraced.

"Have a perfect evening, my darlings. You deserve the very best. Congratulations and best wishes. Good night."

"Why don't you stay for the music and dancing, Mrs. C.?" Greg kissed my cheek.

"Thank you, dear, but I'm coming down with a strange headache. You kids enjoy yourselves. Have a dance for me." I glanced at Enzo, the Romanos' son, set up in a corner with a turntable and a stack of records.

"I love you, Mrs. Carleton." Nadya pulled me closer.

"I love you, sweetheart."

With her porcelain-white complexion and her halo-like garland of daisies, she appeared angelic and vulnerable. I held on to her as tight as I could. She smelled of orange blossoms.

As I slowly climbed the stairs to my apartment, I could hear the tender Beatles song "Here, There, And Everywhere".

* * *

I was removing the copious amount of junk mail from my mailbox when a gangly, blond young man picked up the payphone behind me, dropped a dime and dialed a number.

"It's me...Yeah, I know...It's not that easy." he spoke with a European accent, "Yeah, but, Uncle, those guys are two meters tall...No. Okay."

The hairs on the back of my neck were standing on end. Steve was coming down the stairs. As I glanced up at him, I caught a glimpse of the strange man in my peripheral vision. At the sight of Steve, his phone conversation changed to a language I did not recognize and he swiftly hung up. Before we could observe his appearance, he was out the front door like a shot.

"That's odd." I remarked to Steve.

"I know who that is: Fred's friend Iggy who helped him move. Very interesting. Did he speak any English on the phone before I came down, Mrs. C.?"

"Until he saw you, he was speaking English. He said: 'Those two guys are two meters tall.' He was calling the other person 'Uncle'. Now, I can't tell whether he was his real uncle, or just someone he knows. In a lot of European and Middle-Eastern countries, they call older folks Uncle and Aunt."

"I tell you, Mrs. C., something's very fishy with those two – him and Fred." Steve opened his mailbox.

"He gave me the creeps." I said.

"Don't worry, Mrs. C. I'll get to the bottom of this."

I could not define the feeling of utter sadness engulfing me.

* * *

"You're going to be late for your appointment." she handed him a towel from a hook behind the door.

"When I get back, we can have an encore."

"An encore or two, or three." she winked.

"I love you, Nadya Logan."

"I love you, Greg Logan."

He dressed casually in jeans and a grey bulky sweater, now that he felt more comfortable around Dr. Nicholas.

"Vincent and Joyce are going to stay with you while I'm gone."

"This is so embarrassing, Greg. You can't keep getting our friends to babysit me every time you're out. What are you going to do when you go back to work and you're on nights?"

"By that time, the bad guys'll be in jail."

"What if they're not, honey?"

"They'd better be."

"Seriously, sweetheart, people can't hold my hand like a child. If any bad guys show up, I'll call 911 – okay?"

"You're in danger. Vince and Joyce understand. I've had some long talks with him."

"Be careful yourself." she kissed him, "You're my only reason for living, you know."

"Don't worry about me." he kissed her cheek, "See you soon." he knocked on Vincent's door to let them know he was on his way out.

Vincent and Joyce emerged from his apartment and he waved reassuringly at Greg.

"You'll have to start charging us babysitting fees." Nadya said to Joyce, "Please make yourselves comfortable. I'll make some tea." she closed the door and went into her kitchen, "Both of you'll be fantastic therapists."

"Thank you." he said.

"I hope so." she said.

"You're both empathetic and caring. That's rare. Psychology's in a bad place right now, with too much emphasis on Behavior Modification and a movement away from Humanistic Psychology.

In private practice, you would have control over the type of therapy you use. You're going to heal a lot of broken souls. You two were sent here on a divine mission."

"You're very kind, Nadya." Joyce said.

"Thank you for the vote of confidence." Vincent shifted uncomfortably on the sofa, crossing one leg across the other.

"I'm sorry about the furniture. It's not very comfortable."

"It's not your furniture. Nothing's suited to big guys like me. Greg can relate. When you're well over six feet, and wear size 13 shoes, you have to resign yourself to being uncomfortable. I should've been an athlete, but my interests were elsewhere."

Nadya brought in the tea tray and placed it on the coffee table.

"You've got quite a good assortment of books." he observed, "Psychology, Sociology, Philosophy, Classic Literature..."

"You're multi-faceted." Joyce said.

"I love learning. I did enjoy that aspect of university." Nadya poured tea into three white ceramic cups.

"There are more Psychology books than Sociology books. I thought Sociology was your major." Vincent said.

"I wanted to major in Psychology but I found it too scientific. I struggled with it. Sociology suited my abstract personality."

"Why so many Psychology books, then?"

"I started reading Psychology books when I was eleven. I had this overwhelming compulsion to devour every Psychology book I could get my hands on."

"To try to make sense of your life." Joyce said.

"Yes. To try to understand my parents. I started out trying to understand what was wrong with me, to see if all the stuff they said about me was true. It turned out, all the things they called me were the things they were themselves."

"Doesn't surprise me." he said.

"Mom's a classic Manic Depressive."

"I would've said that, too, from what I've observed."

"She always told me I was mentally unstable."

"I hope you know that you are not."

"I was never sure."

"Take my word for it. They did quite a number on you."

"They called me self-involved for reading Psychology books and for trying to pursue my interests. They called me a selfish ingrate. They seemed to have such an intense, all-consuming contempt for me."

A knock on the door startled Nadya and she spilled her tea on her white turtleneck.

"Nadya, it's Mom."

She froze in panic and gave Joyce a frightened glance.

"Open up, Nadyenka. I heard you got married. Congratulations. Dad's not with me. Mrs. Campbell gave me a ride. She's waiting for me downstairs. I just wanted to drop off a present."

"It's okay." Vincent whispered, "Might as well let her in. We're here."

She opened the door tentatively and stepped outside to prevent her from entering the apartment.

"Aren't you going to invite me in?"

"It's a mess and you know how much you hate a mess."

"Better shape up. If you keep a messy house, you'll lose your handsome new husband."

"He didn't marry me for my housekeeping skills. He married me because he loves me."

"Love! Hmph!" she snickered.

"It may be hard for you to believe anyone could love me, but he really does. Sorry to disappoint you."

"I came all the way here to give you a present, and look how impertinent you are to me!"

"I didn't mean to be. I'm sorry. Thanks for coming by."

"I almost changed my mind about giving this to you. But, then, I remembered you've always had an insufferable personality." Ana handed her an oblong object wrapped in a plastic pantyhose bag folded onto itself.

Nadya studied it for a moment before opening it. A set of six wooden napkin rings were inside the Queen Size pantyhose bag.

"Thank you."

"You know you wouldn't look this ugly if you didn't pluck your eyebrows." Ana said.

"Well, good-bye." Nadya stood in uncertainty.

"Start paying attention to your appearance and hygiene, and clean up your apartment. Try to curb your obnoxious personality." Ana said as she started down the stairs feigning physical pain.

Nadya returned to the apartment and locked the door behind her.

"That was creepy." Vincent shook his head.

"She knows exactly how to push all my buttons." she placed the package on the coffee table.

"She's very jealous of you." Joyce said.

"Me? All her life, she's had hundreds of men pursuing her. She was very beautiful in her youth."

"That's precisely why. You represent her lost youth, lost opportunities, lost hopes. Being the Belle Of The Ball is obviously a high priority for her. She's always known how to work a room, how to charm the men. Aging is not something a narcissist is able to cope with. She has not aged well. That lifestyle takes its toll. She's no longer attracting dozens of admirers. And, here you are: Young, beautiful, loving. She sees you as competition. She's no longer the center of attention. Men are noticing you, instead."

"But I don't do anything to attract men."

"That makes no difference. She's probably noticed men looking at you. Your youth and beauty are enough to create her intense jealousy and contempt. She has Narcissistic Personality Disorder as well as being Manic Depressive."

"I can't deal with it anymore."

"You don't have to. The way you're handling it by limiting contact is the best way to deal with it."

"They keep hounding me."

"They don't want to lose control over you. They want complete control over every aspect of your life."

"It's sick."

"They resent the fact that you now have a support system and people who care about you."

"Isolating me gave them complete power."

"They were able to carry out their brainwashing to destroy your confidence, to crush you completely, to break your spirit. They wanted you to be subservient, alone, and depressed, so they could carry out their torture."

"Thank you for understanding."

"You're welcome." she hugged her, "You've had to deal with their abuse all by yourself for so long. You've been betrayed and traumatized by the people you depended on for love and security, which they were never capable of giving. But you loved them, all the same. You're a loving soul. You had to fight, scratch and claw your way out of the hell they put you through. Your goodness is a threat to them."

Greg turned his key in the lock and Nadya went to the door to greet him.

"How did it go?" Vincent asked Greg.

"Dr. Nicholas feels I'm ready to return to work in January. We have one, maybe two appointments left. How were things around here?"

"We had a visitor." Joyce said, motioning to the coffee table, "And a wedding present for you."

Greg glanced at the pantyhose bag quizzically.

"Everything's all right now. Ana came by earlier to bring that." Vincent said.

"How do they always know when I'm not here?"

"You're going to be back at work soon. You'll smoke them out." Vincent rose, "We'd better get going."

"Thank you, guys." Greg said.

"Thank you." Nadya hugged Joyce.

“Take care of each other.” Joyce waved and followed Vincent to his apartment.

Greg enclosed Nadya in his arms. She was safe and protected. The ghosts of her past could not touch her now. They were locked away in a dark, dusty attic.

Chapter 19/ Tomorrows

The burly man with the greasy, slicked-back dark hair and sunglasses glanced around him nervously in the lobby as he inserted a dime in the payphone and dialed a number.

"It's me...I know. Those two are at it like rabbits day and night over my head. They're driving me bananas. They don't even take time out to eat or sleep...When do we get it done?...That's too long. I'm not sticking around that long...We'll have to have a meeting...There are still details that need to be sorted out."

Noticing Olivia coming in the front door, he called out:

"Hey, Mama, what's cookin'?...Sorry, sir. I just saw a babe and I forgot...Yes sir..." he continued drooling in Olivia's direction, "Right on, sir...I dig it...Roger and out." he hung up and continued leering at Olivia, "Hey, baby, let me show you a good time. You know you want it."

"Go to hell, you scumbag!" Olivia shot him a look of indignation.

"Don't fight it, baby. Let me lick your pussy."

"Drop dead, you disgusting vermin!" she struck him on the head with her briefcase.

"Oooh, that turns me on, baby! A feisty chick! You like it rough? I'll give you rough!"

"Sick pervert!"

"Get out of here now!" Joyce burst into the lobby and berated him.

"No sweat, Mama. Don't get uptight." he slithered away up the stairs to his apartment.

"Are you all right, Liv?" Joyce hugged her.

"We need to get that sick pervert out of this building! You wouldn't believe the things he was saying to me!"

"We'll file a complaint with Sarge tomorrow."

"I don't feel safe knowing that crazed maniac's living in the same building!"

"I know, honey." she patted her on the back, "Come on, let's go to Mama Rosa's for a pick-me-up before we go up."

"Sounds good to me."

Outside, snow was falling in soft, fuzzy flakes in slow motion. They entered the crowded restaurant and were escorted to a cramped table for two in a dark corner, much to their disdain. They ordered two glasses of white wine.

"So, tell me, what's this I hear about you and Vincent?" Olivia nudged her playfully.

Joyce blushed profusely.

"We're taking things very slowly. He's the finest man I've ever met."

"This is the most terrific news I've heard in a long time. I'm very happy for both of you."

"I haven't really dated since my divorce. I've been afraid of getting hurt again. Vincent's very supportive. I feel blessed."

"You deserve it. You're such a nurturing person, Joyce. You need someone sensitive who can appreciate your extraordinary qualities."

"You're going to give me a swelled head, Liv. That's enough about me. How are things going with you and that David fellow?"

"Oh, it fizzled out. He's not into commitment. Too many mind games."

"You'll meet someone who treats you the way you deserve to be treated."

"I'm not in any hurry. If it happens, it happens. If not, c'est la vie. I'm fed up with all the games men play."

"You'll meet the right one. The reason other relationships didn't work was that God was clearing the way for the right one."

"I wish. Thank you for the pep talk."

"Let's get another drink." Joyce attempted to get the waiter's attention.

"Sounds good to me."

After one more drink, Joyce found her thoughts wandering to Vincent and her concentration slipping away from her. When Olivia rose and apologetically informed her she needed to go to Eat-Rite to buy supplies for her supper, she remained at the table alone. As the restaurant grew noisier she decided it was time to go home.

Tortured saxophone music was coming from Vincent's apartment. When she reached the top of the stairs, she walked past her own apartment and knocked on his door. And, he stood there, eyes smoldering. She threw herself into the shelter of his waiting arms. He led her inside and closed the door behind him. She kissed him with an urgency he was unaccustomed to from her.

"Vince, take me to bed now. Make me yours." she spoke hoarsely, burying her face in his chest.

She was unable to meet his gaze. Overcome by a torrent of tears, she shuddered like a captive bird.

"Joyce, you're trembling..." he pressed her close and kissed the top of her fragrant head, "We can wait. You know I can wait as long as you need, until you're ready."

"But I'm ready now."

"Joyce, I want you more than you'll ever know – but not like this. I know this is not the right time for you."

"I've kept you waiting long enough."

"I would wait forever for you, Joyce. But I want to be sure you're ready. There's no rush. We have a lifetime to enjoy each other."

"I didn't want you to be disappointed."

"I could never be disappointed. I'm perfectly content holding you like this." he led her to the sofa.

"Thank you." she placed her head on his shoulder.

"I'm in love with you." he murmured.

"I'm in love with you, too." she closed her eyes.

On the reel to reel tape recorder, Mary Hopkin was singing "Love Is The Sweetest Thing".

* * *

All the street lights were festooned with Christmas decorations. Glittering camels and palm trees formed canopies above the streets. An oddity for December, there was only a scant amount of snow, and mild temperatures. Nadya and Greg came into the lobby, snowflakes clinging to their hair and noses, and Greg's eyebrows.

"Hi, Mrs. Carleton." she embraced me.

"Hi, dear. You two look pretty chipper."

"We're coming back from the doctor." Greg announced, "We're pregnant. Due in August."

"Oh my, congratulations!" I pulled them close.

"You're the first to know."

"I'm very happy for you. I'll treat you to a celebration dinner next week."

"Thank you." she kissed my cheek and he hugged me.

Behind us, Vincent and Joyce were descending the stairs with their arms linked.

"Hey, Vince, my man." Greg called out.

"Hello, folks." Vincent smiled shyly.

"Good to see you both." I said.

"Hello." Joyce's face was beet-red.

"Off to dinner?" Greg asked, "Somewhere nice?"

"The Stardust Room."

"Oooh. Swanky. Have fun. Don't do anything I wouldn't do." Greg raised his eyebrows playfully.

"Greg, there's absolutely nothing you wouldn't do." Vince winked at him, "See you later, folks."

"Bye." Joyce said.

"Have a lovely evening." I said.

"Bye." Nadya called out.

"Mrs. C." Greg said, "Do you have plans for Christmas?"

"No particular plans, dear. Just my usual dinner for one."

"We would like you to spend it with us at my folks' place."

"That's very kind of you, dear. Won't it be an imposition?"

“Not at all. We’re a huge brood. One more person won’t make a difference. Mom roasts four turkeys; she has a double oven. Every sibling brings a side dish or a dessert.”

“What do you think I ought to bring?”

“You don’t have to bring anything, Mrs. C. You’re with us.”

“I’ll bring a dessert.”

“There’s never enough dessert.” he laughed, “I eat everybody else’s share, too.”

“Your pineapple upside down cake is out of this world.” Nadya said.

“All this talk about food is making me hungry.” Greg said, “I’ll treat the three of us to Chinese at Jasmine Garden. How does that sound?”

“Sounds fantastic.” I said.

“Then, let’s go, ladies.” he stood between us and linked his arms through both of ours.

It was a peaceful evening, well-suited for a walk, with no wind, no chill, only tender snowflakes kissing our faces.

“Next week is my very last head-shrinking session.” Greg announced, “They’re going to reinstate me in January, providing they deem my head sufficiently shrunk.”

“That’s so good to hear.” I said.

“I’ll be able to provide for the three of us...Maybe buy a little house for the little one to run around freely in. Nothing fancy. Hopefully, something within walking distance of here.”

“There are nice homes up the hill, past the junior high school.” I said, “There’s a variety of price ranges, too. You could start out with a wartime Cape Cod, move up to a ranch style bungalow.”

“That’s exactly what we were thinking, too.” he said.

“I love Cape Cods.” Nadya smiled.

At that moment, bathing in the innocence of their dreams and the glow of their youthful smiles with the red, green, blue and gold bulbs from the shop windows lighting up their fresh faces, I allowed myself to be deluded into believing nothing and no one could touch them.

* * *

Sandi slipped out of view the moment she caught a glimpse of the unkempt Fred dropping his dime into the payphone.

“It’s me...No, everything’s groovy...That wasn’t what we agreed on...Why does that make a difference?...That’s not what you said before. What am I supposed to do?”

He slammed down the receiver, “Fuck!” he punched the wall beside the phone and stormed out the front door.

Sandi cautiously slipped into the lobby, remaining close to the wall to conceal herself from Fred’s view, who was outside the front door, talking to a blonde woman in a station wagon. She waited until the conversation ended and the woman drove away. When Fred turned around to re-enter the building and made a beeline for the phone, she walked briskly toward the stairs. On the second floor landing, she removed her shoes and tiptoed barefoot to a spot where she could listen to his new phone conversation.

“Listen, you dumbkoff: We’ve got a new customer. Extra bonus with this, too. Heh heh...We’ll talk. See ya.” he hung up.

Sandi raced up the stairs barefoot and unlocked her door, her heart beating like a drum. She stood with her back against the door, breathing deeply.

“Sandi.” she heard Vincent’s voice outside and immediately opened the door.

“Sandi, are you all right? What’s wrong?” he held her shoulders.

“That creepy Fred guy. He’s planning something sinister, making deals over the phone and with some blonde woman in a station wagon. Something is going down. I feel it in my bones. I just got this ominous feeling in my gut.”

“Whatever it is he and his cohorts have up their tattered, soiled sleeves, they won’t be able to pull it off.”

"I hope so."

"He really shook you up, didn't he? That's it. You're coming out to supper with me. I haven't seen much of you lately."

"You've been busy." she winked.

"That reminds me: Joyce has invited both of us for Christmas dinner. I wanted to tell you before she asked you herself. It means a lot to her. Please don't say no."

"No, Vince. Two's company and three's a crowd."

"You're not going to finagle your way out of this one, Ames. She's inviting her brother, too."

"No. No way. Not another matchmaking attempt. You know how I feel about being set up."

"It's not like that. You're my family and he's her family."

"You two really are getting serious. There was a reason you were meant to move here to this obscure corner of the country."

"Kismet." he smiled softly.

"I've waited so long to see you with the right woman. I'm very happy to see you like this."

"Thanks." he said, "Why don't we get caught up over some pizza?"

"Sounds good to me."

Christmas music greeted them as they entered Aphrodite's Pizza, a shabby eatery in a run-down, ugly building two blocks away.

"How did you discover this dive?" she suppressed a laugh.

"Greg brought me here a couple of times. He loves this place."

"Does he actually bring Nadya here?"

"No. It's a guy place."

"That's why you brought me here. Thanks a lot, Green."

"This place reminded me of our days back at Toronto P.D."

"I've got to admit, there is something nostalgic about the place. The questionable clientele is just par for the course. Do they have belly dancers back there or something?"

"Don't worry. They don't."

"Good. Otherwise, I wouldn't be able to keep my food down."

"Where do you want to sit?"

"This table looks as good as any." she selected one near the door.

An emaciated young woman with long, black hair sauntered over to them.

"Whaddaya want?" she asked in a monotonous voice, cracking her gum, one hand on her hip.

"We'd like a large pizza." Vincent said.

"Whaddaya want on it?"

"Sausage, pepperoni, salami, green peppers and onions."

"Whaddaya wanna drink?"

"Sprite for both of us."

Once the young woman was out of earshot, Sandi released the laughter she had been stifling.

"How did you manage to keep a straight face?" she asked him, "Are you even sure it's safe to eat here?"

"The food is actually good." he reassured her.

"Just how drunk were the two of you when you came in here?"

A television set from a back room could be heard over the music, along with children's voices, and an older woman's voice. Following what seemed to be an excruciatingly long time, the young woman returned with their pizza, two white plates, cutlery and two napkins, all of which she placed haphazardly on the table. One plate held two dead flies, which she flicked away nonchalantly. She returned to the back of the restaurant and brought them two cans of Sprite.

Sandi gave Vincent an incredulous look once the woman was gone.

"I'll take that plate." he wiped it with his napkin.

"Greg actually likes this place?"

"He likes rough, old, derelict places." he picked up a slice of pizza and tentatively took a bite, "A bit too hot, but tastes pretty good."

"If you say so." she proceeded to do the same, "Good idea to avoid the cutlery. I see caked-on crud."

"Aren't you glad you came?" he grinned.

"Wouldn't miss this experience for anything in the world."

"I think they're popular with the university students late at night after the bars close."

"Oh, I bet. This is a university student's dream."

"After we leave here, I'll get you a decadent dessert at Mama Rosa's to make up for it."

"Can't wait."

"I miss this."

"Eating in dives?"

"No. Us. Like this."

"Me, too."

"You'll be a terrific lawyer."

"You'll be a terrific therapist."

"I'll always be there for you, Ames."

"I'll always be there for you, too, Green. Now, shut up and eat your pizza, so we can get the heck out of this hellhole!"

Chapter 20/ Fragile

Amid drunken voices delivering an off-key rendition of "Auld Lang Syne", noisemakers going off, and shouts of "Happy New Year!", our group managed to exchange good wishes. I observed from across the restaurant Vincent pulling Joyce into a passionate kiss. In her floor-length cerulean blue crepe dress, she appeared ethereal. I smiled inwardly.

"Happy New Year, Mrs. Logan!" Greg was twirling Nadya in the air.

"Happy New Year, Constable Logan!" she appeared innocent and vulnerable in her simple purple dress.

Arlene and Leroy exchanged an obligatory kiss and remained in their corner with sullen faces, like a long married couple whose marriage was on the fritz. Steve did not appear terribly comfortable, either, with "Kristy The Crustacean" forcing her attention on him in a crude, vulgar manner, groping and pinching. Olivia was on a first date with a professor named Wayne Something-or-another, who was sporting a dark, bushy moustache. He appeared stiff and formal, albeit courteous around her. In her red dress with the plunging neckline, Olivia was a sight to behold. Sandi was having a cordial conversation with a serious-looking middle-aged man, whom she had earlier introduced as Burt Something. Mel and Gayle were making the rounds to every table, socializing with everyone. Steve's widowed uncle and I were attempting to make polite conversation. Enzo put on a tape of instrumental music he himself had compiled. When "Here, There, And Everywhere" began playing, Nadya and Greg were the first on the dance floor. This song was one they both loved, and considered significant to their relationship.

Olivia and Wayne were the first to depart.

"I wonder what he has in store for her." Steve winked at me.

"I hope he doesn't break her heart." I sighed.

"Looks like a real stud." Steve said, on a rare break while Kristy was using the bathroom.

"I'm afraid I'll have to say good night, dear lady." Steve's Uncle Lewis rose to his feet and shook my hand, "It's past my bedtime, and I'm nodding off. I've enjoyed meeting you. I hope we can do this again."

"Likewise."

"Till we meet again, dear lady."

"Bye, Uncle Lew."

"See you later, son."

"Mrs. C., I don't know what to do." Steve whispered, once his uncle had left, "I don't want to go to bed with Kristy, but I don't see how I can get out of it."

"She's a very persistent young woman, isn't she?"

"So aggressive. I don't want to use her. I don't like her and it feels wrong to do the deed. But I'm afraid I have no choice tonight. I can't get out of it."

"I have a feeling she's not the sort of girl you can be up front with about it."

"You can say that again. She's coming back. Wish me luck, Mrs. C."

"Good luck, dear."

Arlene and Leroy stood and walked out of the restaurant. Neither returned, and it was obvious they were headed in separate directions. Steve and Kristy were arguing. She stormed out, with him in pursuit. He returned shortly without her.

"That did not go well." he said.

"When she calms down, she'll understand."

"I feel like a heel, Mrs. C. I didn't want to hurt her feelings."

"She'll see that once she's calmer and more sober."

"I hope so."

"Don't worry, dear."

Mel and Gayle were the next ones to leave. Sandi's companion bade her good night and she went upstairs to her apartment.

I smiled at the sight of Joyce and Vincent dancing to the hauntingly beautiful "Greenfields". Nadya and Greg watched them with beaming faces.

"I'll walk you to your door, Mrs. C." Steve took my arm after the song ended and both couples departed.

* * *

They stood awkwardly outside her door. She removed her key from her beaded clutch purse and unlocked her door. Glancing up at his glistening brown eyes, she smiled and stroked his soft cheek.

"Thank you for the lovely evening."

"Thank you for the pleasure of your company." he leaned in for a shy, tender kiss.

She drew him nearer and kissed him with fervor.

"Would you like to come in for a drink?" she murmured.

He nodded and followed her into the apartment. She switched on the ceiling light.

"What would you like to drink?"

"Just a soft drink. Anything you have."

"I have Perrier. Is that all right?" she opened the cupboard and removed two glasses.

"More than all right." he followed her to the kitchen.

She opened the avocado green fridge, took out one of the tall, slender bottles of Perrier, and poured its contents into the glasses on the counter. He was standing behind her. She could feel his breath on her neck and shoulders. Her heart in her throat, she turned around. He pulled her into his arms. Surrendering to his kisses, she sighed under his touch, her desire for him growing more urgent. He unzipped her dress and loosened his tie. She took his hand and led him to the bedroom.

"Are you sure?"

"I've never been more sure of anything in my life." she said, tears shining in her eyes.

Her unzipped dress fell to the floor with one twist of her shoulders. She stepped out of her shoes and dress. He tossed his suit coat and tie. Unbuttoning his shirt, she buried her face in his chest, and covered him with feverish kisses. He unclasped her bra, pulled it off her savagely, allowing his fingers to explore her breasts. His shirt found its way to the pile on the floor. She unbuckled his belt, unzipped his pants and caressed him from his chest to his knees. He grabbed at the layers of elastic around her waist and desperately tore her half-slip, pantyhose and panties off her. The touch of his fingers sent shivers through her. She stood before him, vulnerable and exposed. Free from the shackles of his remaining articles of clothing, he pressed her close to him and kissed her wildly. She moaned in yearning. They fell on the bed, their mouths devouring each other. It felt so right to have his weight crushing her like this. He smoothly found his way home. He was where he belonged. He enclosed her in the shelter of his arms until they both fell asleep.

She awakened to the first fingers of dawn and kept her head on his chest. Both of them had waited so long for this. She moved slightly to watch him sleeping, his long, dark eyelashes resting on his cherubic cheeks, his pouty mouth open. The rhythm of his breathing vibrated in her chest. He stirred and instinctively reached for her in his sleep. She kissed his long delicate hand. Until now, the last man – and the first, and everything in between, had only been Eugene. They had known each other forever, grown up together. He had been her only boyfriend. They had married young and settled into their teaching careers. Turning forty had not been a smooth transition for Eugene. He had traded in his old sedan for a flashy Mustang and traded her in for a young, leggy nurse. In all their years of marriage, Eugene had never made her feel the way Vincent did. Vincent stirred again and opened his eyes.

"Hi there, pretty lady." he smiled.

"Hi there, yourself." she smiled back.

It was exhilarating to awaken to him beside her.

"Do you know how lovely you are?" he kissed her.

"You're the good-looking one." she stroked his cheek.

"Are you kidding me? You look like the Champagne Lady from Lawrence Welk."

"I'm definitely no Norma Zimmer, but I'll be your Champagne Lady, if you want."

"Why did we wait this long?" he played with her hair, "Why did I waste so much time?"

"You needed some healing time, Vincent. You were coming off a bad relationship. Healing is a lengthy process."

"I had my head stuck in the sand. I almost let you get away."

"I wasn't going anywhere. You found me."

"Now that I've found you, I'll never let you go."

"Never let me go."

He reached under the covers and caressed her. His lips brushed over her eyelids, cheeks, nose, lips, neck, and fell on her breasts. His fingers were moving between her legs, sending ripples of ecstasy right through to her core. His hands seemed to know every inch of her as though they had always been lovers.

As the sun rose and slithered in through the slats of the window blinds in ribbons of light, the two of them held each other like castaways on an unknown land.

Chapter 21/ Greenfields

He studied her blonde eyelashes resting on her flawless fair skin, her blonde, delicately arched eyebrows, her tiny, doll-like features, and strands of golden hair falling across her soft cheek as she slept beside him. He thought about how exquisitely she had given herself to him, how graceful she was in everything she did. Waking up beside her was a privilege never to be taken for granted. He wanted her more than he had ever wanted anyone.

It made more sense for the two of them to be together at his apartment. She had been embarrassed about being heard by their neighbors. His place was tucked away in the back, out of the path of foot traffic and relatively protected from street noise. His immediate neighbors were also not as much cause for concern. Greg and Nadya's own lovemaking was loud enough to wake the dead. There was plenty of space in his closet for her clothes, and abundant storage room in the kitchen for her supplies.

He arranged the covers around her shoulders, and gazed at her tenderly. She stirred and reached for him, her hand searching for his arm and resting on it ever so softly. He loved watching her sleep like this. Her eyes opened and she smiled groggily.

"Hi."

"Hi." he smiled and touched the tip of her nose.

"Have you been awake long?"

"Not too long." he gazed at her with adoring eyes.

"I was just dreaming about us." she smiled.

"I hope it was a happy dream." he stroked her hair.

"We were running through fields of daisies – just like the song: The lovers in Greenfields."

"Our song." his index finger traced a line from her hip to her knee.

"It really is our song. The title is our last names together."

His eyes glistening with tears, he kissed her forehead.

Her mouth was pressed against his upper arm. He felt soft, warm and moist. He released his hold to look at her face. She ran a fingertip over his eyelids, his cheeks, nose and lips. He took her hand and kissed it. His hands on her cheeks, he brushed his lips across her face, his tears blending with hers.

"Please don't ever leave me." he whispered, "I can't live without you."

"I would never, ever leave you. I would rather die than live without you. I love you." she kissed his soft pillowy lips.

"I love you so much."

Her fingers deftly danced through his gently greying curls, across his back, and on the soft roundness of his buttocks. His lips moved lower until they found the spot he so cherished. Every movement of his tongue drove her to the brink of madness. She pulled at his hair and screamed so loud, her throat hurt. As her heart exploded, he enveloped her in his arms until her quivering and tears subsided.

"I want to cherish every single moment with you." he said.

"I never want to be away from you."

They remained there, bathed in the cold glare of the winter sun.

* * *

They stood beside her white Chevelle in the parking lot, kissing.

"Drive carefully." he stroked her hair, "I wish you didn't have to meet with your supervisor today."

"I'll try to get away as soon as I can, honey. You can get a lot more work done on your thesis if I'm not here to distract you."

"Who cares about my thesis?" he kissed her again, "I don't want a single minute away from you."

She held his face in her hands and kissed him long and hard.

"Hey, get a room, you two!" Mel teased as he and Gayle walked by them.

"Woo hoo!" Steve whistled, "Hello, young lovers!"

"Don't waste your breath, guys! They can't even hear you." Gayle laughed.

"Ain't love grand!" Greg patted Vincent on the back.

Nadya and Olivia walked by, smiling. Arlene hummed the theme song from "Romeo and Juliet".

"I think I'd better go." Joyce pulled away.

"I smudged your lipstick." Vincent said apologetically.

She removed a tissue from her handbag and handed it to him. He wiped off smudges of peach lipstick from her face.

"I'll have a tuna casserole waiting when you get home." he said, "If I burn it, I'll get some lasagna from Mama Rosa's."

"I love you, my handsome prince." she stroked his cheek.

"I love you, my Champagne Lady." he took her hand and kissed it.

As she drove away, he stood like a lost child whose mother had left him alone on the first day of kindergarten. Hanging his head, he returned to the front of the building and entered the restaurant. He took a table in a corner and ordered a black coffee.

"Why so glum? You know she's coming back." Sandi sat across the table from him.

"Love has changed me so much. I've gone through life being completely self-sufficient, never allowing myself to get too close emotionally. Now, I meet the most incredible woman on earth and melt into mush. You knew before I did that Joyce and I were meant for each other. Being a guy, I'm stupid about this stuff."

"In the past, all my talks with you involved warning you about protecting your heart from the women you were meeting. I'm finding myself doing a complete 180 this time: Don't mess this up, Green. Don't hurt her. Don't break her tender heart. You're the luckiest guy on earth to be loved by Joyce. The woman is a saint."

"I realize how blessed I am. I can't even believe she wants to be with me. I'd rather die than do anything to hurt her."

"Hold on to her. Don't ever let her go."

"I can't imagine my life without her."

"Just treat her right. If you hurt her, you'll answer to me. I've got to get going." she stood up, "By the way, don't take her to Aphrodite's!"

* * *

She threw her arms around him the moment he opened the door.

"I heard your footsteps." he told her, pressing her close, "I missed you so much, I opened the closet and smelled your clothes."

"I missed you, too." she kissed him.

He took her handbag and briefcase from her. Then, he removed her white wool coat and hung it up in the closet as she unzipped her white snow boots.

"It smells so nice here." she said.

"I didn't burn the casserole. I followed your recipe right down to the letter." he turned on the stereo console and pressed the button to play the reel to reel tape. Beverly Bremers' song "Don't Say You Don't Remember" filled the room.

"I love this song so much." she gazed adoringly at him.

"I know that. I made a tape with your favorites: All the melancholy music I know you love."

"Thank you. You're spoiling me."

"You deserve to be spoiled. You deserve to be treated like a queen."

"I love you so much, it hurts. I can't believe we're together like this."

"Believe it. Let me prove it to you."

"You do, each and every day, in everything you do."

"I have our food set to the timer, so it can turn itself off. We can work up an appetite in the meantime." he led her to the bedroom.

Her eyes glistening and overcharged, she unbuttoned his grey flannel shirt and buried her face in his chest. He unbuttoned her suit jacket and tossed it on the chair. Her delicate white blouse revealed a subtle glimpse of the white lace bra underneath. Slowly and deliberately, he released the pearl buttons of her blouse, savoring the texture of her skin through the spaces between the buttons. The final button undone, he reached under the blouse to caress her. He unzipped her skirt and let it fall to the floor. He knelt at her feet, wrapped his arms around her legs and rested his head against his sacred place. Her heart leaping out of her chest, she lowered herself to the floor and wrapped her legs around him. Breathless, mad with desire, they devoured one another. He savagely tore her undergarments. She thought her heart would stop. When he collapsed beside her in the afterglow, the tape was playing Todd Rundgren's "I Saw The Light (In Your Eyes)", the popular hit song from two years earlier, written in a minor key. They lay on the floor, listening.

"What was your impression of me before we got better acquainted?" he asked.

"...That you were deep, complex, and reserved. I didn't think you'd ever be interested in me...You next: What was your impression of me?"

"That you were exquisite and fragile. I was afraid to approach you."

"I'm glad you did."

"So am I. I also thought you would be more conventional."

"Conventional?" she laughed.

"I thought you'd rebuff me...You know: 'I'm not ready to take our relationship to that level yet.', or the other usual stuff. I had no idea you were such a wild woman."

"Now I'm a wild woman, am I?"

"You hide your light under a bushel."

"So do you."

"I thought you'd be more conventional in bed, too."

"You were doing an awful lot of thinking, weren't you?"

"You're so shy and demure...I didn't think you'd be so passionate."

"If you thought I was so 'conventional', why did you want to get to know me, then? Perhaps, I answered my own question. You initially had no interest in me."

"Joyce, I wanted to be with you long before I ever spoke a word to you. I found you mesmerizing."

"You're such a charmer." she tickled him under his chin.

The tape started playing "Early In The Morning" by the British group "Vanity Fare", with the clever play on the spelling.

"I have to tell you: I was so relieved to find out that you don't wear a suit of armor like other women."

"Suit of armor!" she burst into laughter.

"That stuff must be bullet-proof."

"Bullet-proof!" her face turned crimson from laughter.

"Why do they wear them?"

"Because women are brainwashed into believing it is not acceptable to have natural curves. Those foundation garments literally squeeze every ounce of flesh into a rigid tube to form an unnatural shape. They're hot, uncomfortable, and unhealthy. I wear clothes that don't cling to my body, so I won't have to wear those implements of torture."

"I love all your curves just the way they are." he caressed her hips, "I love that you're so natural. There's no pretense, no prudish stuff, nothing artificial. You're not afraid to show you're human. What you see is what you get."

"Those are the qualities I love so much about you. You are true to yourself. You are a remarkable man."

His arms enclosed her again. The tape was playing "Greenfields". She did not want to get dressed just yet. She did not want to wash off any part of Vincent from her body. Her legs were pleasantly wet and she wanted them to remain that way for as long as possible. He stood up and put on his clothes. He lifted her up effortlessly. She wrapped her white chenille robe around herself and followed him to the kitchen.

Chapter 22/ Beginnings

January remained merciful to us. No temperatures below minus thirteen degrees Fahrenheit, no brutal winds, only our garden variety blizzards.

The day of Joyce and Vincent's wedding was a crisp, sunny day with pristine snowbanks, glittering ice crystals, and a cloudless sky. We held the reception at Mama Rosa's at five o'clock. They had a civil ceremony with Sandi and Peter, Joyce's brother, as witnesses. I observed them from the window of the restaurant, returning on foot, Joyce in a long, regal white hooded coat with white fur trim. Her golden hair framed her delicate face in corkscrew curls. Vincent was dashing as always in black.

"They're like a fairy tale couple." Arlene remarked, peering out from her seat on the yellow painted radiator.

"You're the one who caught Nadya's bouquet." Steve said, "But Joyce is the one getting married."

"I'm so happy for her, Steve." Arlene beamed, "She deserves this more than anyone."

"You'd better get in there and catch this bouquet, too." Steve said, "You'll need the extra reinforcement to light a fire under old Leroy."

"I won't hold my breath."

"Here we are again, Mrs. C." he turned to me, "Another wedding here at The Splendid."

"Indeed. I wonder who'll be next."

"Arlene."

"I hope so, too."

"Don't hold your breath." Arlene said, "I have a feeling the next wedding's going to be yours, Steve." she winked, "Kristy just rented Joyce's old apartment. She's moving in the first of February."

"Perish the thought. I hope you're pulling my leg."

"Nope. Got it straight from the horse's mouth."

"Nooo."

"'Fraid so, chum."

"I'm getting a roommate, then." he said.

"That won't keep her away. She'll just wait till he's out."

"I'll get a female roommate!" he beamed, "I amaze myself when I come up with these brainstorms!"

"How is that going to be a deterrent for Kristy? She's going to think you two are an item and back off? Dream on."

"Desperate times call for desperate measures."

"Why don't you try to fix Kristy up with a guy who can take her off your hands?"

"I don't hate any guy enough to do that to him. You'd better get over there quick and catch the bouquet!"

When Arlene joined the others across the restaurant, Steve sat down beside me.

"I need earplugs living right under those two, Mrs. C. I hope I'm that good when I'm Vince's age."

"I don't think you'll have any cause for concern in that department, dear." I patted him on the shoulder.

Cameras were capturing the blissful occasion. Joyce's brother Peter did not miss a single moment, a single expression, a single angle with his camera. In her elegant but simple white dress, Joyce was the epitome of grace and serenity.

"What is it with you and weddings, Mrs. C.?" Steve said, "You look pale and tired again."

"You're very observant, Steve. I think I'm getting overly emotional and it's taking its toll on me. I love both of these couples so dearly."

"You're a very special lady, Mrs. C."

Across the restaurant, Arlene was engaged in a conversation with Olivia, who was holding the bouquet of white carnations and baby's breath. Steve's eyes were betraying his heart.

"You have it bad for her." I said.

"If I could have one dying wish, it would be to spend one night with Olivia."

"I am not going to be one of those people who spout clichés and urge you to tell her how you feel. That is not always a good idea. Only you can know whether or not it's the right thing to do. In my youth, I found myself humiliated beyond belief the few times I confessed my feelings to men. They were terribly uncomfortable and shunned me afterwards. One was actually horribly cruel and callous. Sometimes our hearts fall for people who are wrong for us and following our hearts brings us nothing but pain. Only our heads can give us clarity over the follies of our foolish hearts."

"I agree with you, Mrs. C." he continued to gaze pensively in her direction.

Enzo put on Beverly Bremers' record, and Joyce and Vincent took to the dance floor. Soon, the guests followed suit. Sandi was dancing with Peter. I smiled inwardly. Olivia and Arlene appeared to have decided to blend in with the other guests, not allowing their lack of dates to be a deterrent. Continuing their conversation, they stiffly slow danced with each other, the bouquet still securely in place in Olivia's hand.

"May I have this dance, Mrs. C.?" Steve took my hand.

Not so subtly, he led me beside Arlene and Olivia, and cut in. Arlene and I found ourselves dancing with each other.

"Pretty slick." Arlene said, "He wouldn't have the nerve to cut in like that if she were dancing with a man."

"I hope she's nice to him." I said.

The music had changed to Louis Armstrong's "What A Wonderful World". Arlene led me to a group of chairs with a view of the dance floor and the surrounding tables.

"She's actually engaging in a conversation with him." she reassured me, "Things are looking up for Steve."

"Appears that way."

"Do you know where Joyce and Vincent are going on their honeymoon, Mrs. C.?"

"Niagara Falls, I think."

"Everybody goes to Niagara Falls. If I ever get married, I'd want to go somewhere different. I don't know where. Just a different place. I thought they'd never do anything other people do."

"They'll find a way to make the experience uniquely their own. I can't see them frequenting souvenir shops or other tourist attractions."

"They won't leave their room the whole time, anyway, knowing those two." Arlene winked.

Enzo was playing Don Goodwin's "This Is Your Song". It seemed to cause an intense reaction from Olivia. Steve placed his hand over hers and led her to a nearby table. We watched them as they ordered drink after drink. Steve switched to 7Up, but Olivia continued ordering cocktails.

"She's knocking back those Singapore Slings pretty fast." I observed.

"She's pretty bummed out. Wayne just dumped her."

"That poor lamb. I don't understand the way some men behave these days." I shook my head.

"That was our song – mine and Wayne's." a red-eyed Olivia wiped her nose on her cocktail napkin.

"Olivia, please don't do this to yourself. He's not worth it."

"You're right. He's not worth it. Let's have another drink."

"Olivia, I think you've had enough to drink already."

"No, it's never enough. I need another drinky-poo. Come on, be a sweetheart and get me another one, Stevie."

"You've had enough. I'm going to get you some black coffee."

"You're no fun. Fine. I'll get it myself." she attempted to stand up, however, stumbled, and fell into Steve's arms.

"Come on. I'll take you upstairs and make you coffee." he kept one arm around her, and with his free hand, picked up the bouquet from the table.

"Yes, Mommy." she giggled.

"She took it hard, poor kid." Arlene said, "You'd think a gorgeous girl like Olivia would get everything she wants, but it's just the opposite. The men she meets seem to resent her for being so beautiful and treat her like crap."

"They feel insecure about their own manhood, so they resent the object of their desire." I said.

As "Greenfields" began to play, the crowd cheered "Mr. and Mrs. Greenfield!", and crowded around the couple.

"I like the way they combined their last names." Arlene said, "How amazing is that? Even their names fit together to form the title of their favorite song. All the stars must've been aligned to bring them into each other's lives."

"I'm afraid I'm a little tired, Arlene, dear. I hope you'll excuse me if I go upstairs."

"No problem, Mrs. C. I'm kind of bushed myself, being on my feet all day. I was thinking of going up, too."

We wished the bride and groom well. My temples began throbbing as I held them in my arms.

"Thank you, Mrs. C." Joyce kissed my cheek, "I love you."

"I love you very much, dear."

Vincent kissed my other cheek. As Arlene and I walked out of the restaurant, my head was about to burst open.

* * *

Steve opened her door for her and turned on her lights. He placed the bouquet on the coffee table. Olivia stepped out of her shoes and headed for the hutch in the corner of the congested living room. She attempted to extract a bottle of brandy from the bottom of the cabinet. Steve intercepted, pulled her hand out and shut the cabinet door.

"What you need is black coffee, and I'm going to make you some." he led her to the sofa and turned on the television, "Let's find a nice show you can watch while I make coffee."

He changed the channels by turning the dial among the four available channels.

"We have "All In The Family", "Streets Of San Francisco", "Happy Days", and "The Waltons". What's your preference?"

"I don't want anything happy."

"Okay. We'll scrap "Happy Days", then. How about "The Waltons"? There's an Olivia in it."

"I don't want to see another Olivia living a better life than mine."

"Okay, then. We've got only two choices left. Which one?"

""Streets Of San Francisco". I want to see some blood and gore, murder and mayhem. Seeing that perky, cute blonde on "All In The Family" getting all kissy-faced with her hippie husband would make me puke."

""Streets Of San Francisco" it is, then." he changed it to the right channel.

"I don't want to watch any syrupy, lovey-dovey stuff. Give me a good old-fashioned cop show any day."

"A girl after my own heart."

"Why are you so nice to me, Steve?"

"Because I'm crazy about you."

"That's not a good idea. You shouldn't be crazy about me."

"Why would you say that?"

"Because I'm a mess."

"Olivia, you're not a mess."

"Look at me: Forty-two years old, and still getting used and abused by men."

"That's not a reflection on you, but them. There's something wrong with them. Any guy who doesn't see what a special lady you are is an idiot. Where do you dig up these psychos, anyway?"

"They're all English Profs."

"Well, that explains everything." he laughed.

"And they're all narcissists, perverts, and duplicitous scumbags!"

"Why would you even give them the time of day? When English Profs ask you out, you should run the other way as fast as you can."

"That's exactly what I'm going to do from now on!"

"Why didn't you date Psych Profs? It would seem to be an obvious choice, since you're a Psych student."

"Because they're all nice, fatherly family men – not Casanovas like English Profs."

"Oh, okay. It all makes sense now."

"I honestly thought Wayne was different. He wasn't a bad person...but in a way, he hurt me more."

"He didn't deserve you."

"Steve, thank you."

"For what?"

"Cheering me up."

"I'm glad I could be useful. I'd better make that coffee."

"Forget about the coffee." she stood and wound her arms around his neck, "Why don't you stay with me tonight?"

"Olivia..."

"Come on. Don't leave me alone."

"I don't want to take advantage of you."

"You wouldn't be taking advantage of me, because I'm taking advantage of you, silly." she giggled.

"Olivia, you're not yourself. This is the booze talking."

"Booze. Let's have more booze."

"You've had more than enough. You need coffee. You watch Michael Douglas and I'll make coffee."

"Party pooper." she pouted, but obeyed him.

When he returned with her coffee, she motioned him to sit beside her.

"How're things with you and Arlene's cousin, Whatchamacallit?" she asked.

"Kristy The Crustacean." he frowned.

"Kristy The Crustacean! I love it!" she laughed.

"She's like a bad rash. Can't get rid of her."

"Bad rash!" she squeezed his elbow, "She's mucho annoying, isn't she? Relentless in her pursuit of you."

"She pursues anything that moves. I wish I had moved faster in the opposite direction."

"You know, if Kristy were a fictitious character, all the critics would say she wasn't developed very well, and was coming off as a one-dimensional stock character. What all those literary snobs don't realize is that real people can be much more shallow than fictitious ones. Those pricks don't have a clue what the real world is like. They live in their insular, protected cocoons, indulge in every hedonistic pleasure with no regard for other people's feelings. Then, they have the audacity to critique the writings of people who have truly suffered and experienced the real world, who have been to hell and back, who still carry wounds inflicted by pricks like them."

"Amen to that."

"They sleep with their students and do drugs with them. They're amoral and despicable."

"No arguments from me."

"Let's drink to that." she held up her coffee mug, tears streaming down her face.

"Hey, it's going to be okay." he moved closer to her.

"It's not just what they did to me...They destroy everything they touch. They ruin lives."

"They can't hurt you anymore."

She lifted her eyes to his face. Her black mascara and eyeliner were running down her face in long parallel streaks, giving her the appearance of a sad harlequin.

Then, she kissed him. She tasted like wedding cake and smelled of alcohol and Chanel #5. He responded the way she expected him to. She ripped his tie off his neck and unbuttoned his shirt frantically.

"Olivia...We can't do this..." he said hoarsely.

"I thought you wanted me."

"I do. You can't imagine how much...But not like this."

"I want you to stay with me tonight. I don't want to be alone."

"When the booze wears off, you'll feel different. I should leave before we do something we'll both regret." he sprang to his feet.

"If you leave, I'll drink again."

"That's not fair."

"And it's not fair that you don't want to stay with me."

"Olivia, I do. I want to be with you. That's just the problem."

"I don't see a problem." she stood shakily and placed her hands on his shoulders.

"You'll get your pretty dress all wrinkled."

"No problem."

Her ruffled bohemian georgette dress fell to the floor. She stood in her black silk teddy.

"Holy shit, Olivia! What are you doing to me?"

"Don't fight it, Steve." she gyrated her hips.

All he could see was the pain in her eyes, and the lost little girl behind the beautiful woman. He reached out to hold her.

"I am going to stay with you tonight, Olivia." he kissed her forehead, "But I am not going to take advantage of your inebriated state. I'm just going to hold you."

She placed her head on his shoulder. Nestled in the safety of his arms, she wept like a child.

Chapter 23/ Shannon

"Looks like there's a lot less stuff coming out than there was going in." Jim observed.

"I sold most of my stuff, Jim. They were remnants of my old life. Now that I'm starting a new life, I didn't want any reminders of the past."

"I hope you'll be very happy with your new husband."

"Thank you."

"Word on the street is, your ex-husband is splitsville with his new lady. Yep. She's taking him to the cleaners, too. He has to sell the house and split the profits with her. That was your house and his together. He had no right to keep it after your divorce. He was the guilty one."

"His lawyer just happened to be more dishonest than mine."

"Well, he sure is finally getting what he had coming to him now. What goes around comes around."

"I have no ill will toward Eugene, Jim. It's all water under the bridge. I would never have met Vincent if Eugene hadn't done what he did. He ended up doing me a favor by setting me free."

"You're one classy lady, Joyce. Don't know too many people who'd say that."

"Thanks, Jim. Sometimes, bad things happen to clear the way for good things to find us."

"That's a real nice way of looking at it...You're only taking these boxes here? What about the living room set?"

"It's staying. The little girl who's renting the apartment wanted it, so her dad bought it for her. It was just another reminder of the old house. Once Vince and I buy a place of our own, we'll get all new, fresh things."

"Sounds like a good plan. Where are the boxes going?"

"Peter said I could store them in his finished basement until Vince and I buy a house. He has an empty bedroom there."

"Wise decision. Will he be there to let us in?"

"He's expecting you."

"I'll get right on it." he stacked two large boxes and lifted them, "I'll send Ernie up for the others."

"I'd better pay you now, then."

"No. Your money's no good with us. I'm not charging you for a few boxes, and odds and ends."

"Please, Jim. Let me at least pay for the gas."

"I won't hear of it." he started down the stairs, leaving her standing in the hallway, stunned.

* * *

Arlene opened her door to catch a glimpse of Steve tiptoeing out of Olivia's apartment.

"Gotcha!" she called out.

"Don't do that!" he stumbled, tripping over his own feet.

"Somebody got lucky last night."

"Shh..." he pressed his finger to his lips.

"Guilty conscience?" she winked.

"Nothing happened."

"Sure, Steve. I believe you."

"I'm serious, Arlene."

"Sure. I just fell off the turnip truck yesterday."

"I didn't want to take advantage of Olivia in her state."

"You're cracking me up."

Nadya and Greg's door was opened tentatively and Nadya appeared.

"Hi, guys. Sorry to interrupt." she said, "I heard you talking out here and I caught Olivia's name being mentioned. I was just wondering if she was okay."

"Steve can tell you how she is." Arlene smirked, "In graphic detail."

"Cut it out, Arlene."

"She didn't look well when you two left last night." Nadya said, "I was worried about her. That professor did a real number on her."

"She's sleeping it off." Steve said, "When she wakes up, she could use a friend."

"I'll try her later, then."

"Steve's got to sleep it off, too." Arlene said, "He had a busy night."

"Nothing happened." he said firmly.

"You guys can continue the debate. I've got to get to work." Arlene said, "Some of us unfortunately have to work Saturday mornings."

"Greg's working today, too."

"I have to work tonight."

"I saw Mel and Gayle going off to work from my window a while ago." Arlene said.

"Mel wants to move up the ranks to detective, and Gayle wants to train as a paramedic. She's been a 911 operator so long, she's feeling burnt out." Steve said.

"The only thing I'm working toward is owning my own shop." Arlene said.

"All my hopes and career plans are abstract, intangible pipe dreams." Nadya said, "The most important thing for me is being married to Greg and raising this baby." She patted her abdomen, "I can't wait till May, so I can wear maternity clothes."

"As for Steve, we all know what his plans and dreams are...Ahem." Arlene said, locking her door and starting toward the stairs, "See you guys later."

"Bye, Arlene." Nadya said.

"Bye, Big Mouth." Steve grimaced and turned to Nadya, "I was with Olivia all night, but I didn't take advantage of her."

"I know you genuinely care about her. You'd never do anything to hurt her."

"Thank you."

"Arlene knows that, too. She just can't resist ribbing you."

"I appreciate that. I'd better try to catch forty winks before I go to work tonight."

Nadya's eyes fell on Vincent and Joyce's door and she smiled fondly. Olivia emerged from her apartment and beamed when she saw Nadya.

"Olivia! I was going to ask you to come over." she hugged her.

"I'd love that." she locked her door and put her key in her jean pocket.

Nadya put on the tea kettle as Olivia curled up on the sofa.

"I really made a fool of myself last night." Olivia said.

"No, you didn't."

"I did. I drank way too much. Now I'm so hung over, I can't see straight."

"Can I get you anything?"

"Just company. I don't need anything else."

"I'm always here for you." she returned to the room, sat beside her and placed her hand over hers.

"I feel like a total idiot."

"Olivia, I'm sure there isn't one person at that reception who hasn't had too much to drink at one time or another. Besides, you're always classy and lovely. Last night was no exception."

"You always make me feel better."

"You've been there for me many times."

"I really did make a mess of things after the reception. Steve brought me home. I literally threw myself at him. But he didn't take me up on it. He was honorable."

"He really cares about you, Olivia."

"Nadya, what is wrong with me? I keep losing my head over the worst men, who don't give a damn about me, use me, and throw me away. Then, I totally overlook a good guy who treats me like royalty."

"The bad ones are very clever and skillful at the game of seduction."

"Sometimes we miss what's right under our noses because we're too busy playing the fool for people who don't deserve a single moment of our time."

"Maybe last night was a revelation."

"It opened my eyes to the way I've been setting myself up for heartbreak all my life. I just wish I hadn't made such a spectacle of myself."

"You were among friends. No one was judging you, Olivia." she stroked her hair.

"How can I face Steve again?"

"The two of you need to have a heart to heart talk."

Olivia buried her head in her hands.

"It's going to be all right." Nadya patted her shoulder.

"I can't face him."

"Yes you can. Once you sit down and start talking, all the words will fall into place."

"All this time, I thought of him as just a kid. I underestimated him. He's ten times more mature than men twice his age."

"He's a very nice guy."

"I'm forty-two, and he's...what...twenty-five? That makes me a cradle snatcher."

"Who cares about age? Chronological age is just a random number. It's the age of our souls that matter. He came into your life for a reason."

"But living in the concrete, merciless world, can we make it last in spite of all the obstacles?"

"Don't worry about the future. Enjoy what feels right. If it doesn't last, it doesn't mean it was wrong. It just means it was meant to be for that period of time and under those circumstances. Enjoy the gift you've been given."

"I need to make it up to him for the way I've behaved."

"He understands."

"I feel a lot better now. Thank you." Olivia said, "Did Joyce and Vincent leave yet for their honeymoon?"

"Just a little while ago. Joyce's mover took her stuff to Peter's house earlier, so the apartment would be ready for Kristy."

"Kristy the crustacean." Olivia rolled her eyes, "I hope her stay here isn't a long one."

"She'll be gone soon. She's a flake anyway. Let's have some of this strawberry tea and blueberry muffins."

Olivia followed her to the kitchen and wiped her tears with a paper towel. Her smile met Nadya's. On this icy winter morning, she felt the warmth of a summer sun in this tiny apartment.

* * *

"What's all this commotion downstairs?" Kristy wanted to know.

"I didn't notice anything." Arlene kept her eyes on the television.

"It sounds like stuff being moved."

"Oh that. It's just Steve's roommate."

"I didn't know he was getting one. Besides, he's only subletting. Can he even do that?"

"It hasn't been a sublet for months. His name's on the lease. After Greg came back to town and moved in with Nadya, he put his name on the lease with her and turned his old apartment over to Steve."

"But it's only a one bedroom like all the other apartments."

"There's plenty of room."

"What's his roommate's name?"

"Shannon."

"When do I meet him?"

"At the Valentine's Day party at Mama Rosa's."

"Fine. See you there, then. Seeing as you're more interested in watching T.V. anyway, I'll leave." Kristy scowled, unnoticed by Arlene, "I have to go to Eat-Rite, anyway."

"See ya."

Arlene wondered what would happen at the party when all the cards were laid out on the table. There was a knock at her door. Had Kristy forgotten something? Then, she heard a reassuring voice.

"Arlene, it's me, Sandi."

Arlene turned off "Gilligan's Island" and opened the door.

"Hi. I wanted to return your cookbook and your nail polish."

"Come on in. Your nails look gorgeous." she admired her tastefully trimmed and subtly polished peach nails.

"Thanks for letting me borrow it. I normally never do girly stuff, but I really love the look of this. I might buy some myself."

"That's good to hear. Just make sure it's Revlon, though. Stay away from the cheaper brands. Revlon's pricey, but it's the best. The salons only use Revlon."

"Thanks. And, I wrote down some of the less difficult recipes from your book. As you can tell, I'm not a natural when it comes to domestic stuff. I nearly failed Home Economics."

"Cookbooks try to make recipes harder than they need to be. You can modify them to make things much easier on yourself."

"I made Chicken A La King for tonight. Peter's coming over for supper."

"Oooh. Things are heating up." Arlene winked.

"I haven't really dated since my husband Hugh was murdered ten years ago."

"Oh, I'm sorry." Arlene blushed.

"He was killed in the line of duty. He was a police officer."

"I'm sorry, Sandi. I'm glad you're seeing Peter now."

"He's very nice. He's been widowed for about five years, so we do have that in common."

"What does he do for a living?"

"He's a chemist at Organic Research Facility."

"I hope it works out for you, Sandi. I guess I'll see you two at the party."

"This party promises to be a very interesting evening for certain people."

"You can say that again."

"Is Leroy coming?"

"So he says. He probably won't show up. I'm getting fed up with the way he takes me for granted. I'm thinking of withholding my affections. I used to be afraid that would make him stray, but now I think I've been too accommodating. I've wasted my best years on him. Now I think I should've held out for marriage before having relations with him. He would've treated me better if I had been less accommodating."

"That depends on the man. Leroy seems like the old-school type with chauvinistic attitudes. He's not worth holding on to if he doesn't appreciate you, Arlene. You deserve more out of a relationship."

"You're right. I've been with just one guy all my life, since I was sixteen. We didn't have relations until our twenties, and I only gave in because I thought we had a future together. It didn't occur to me he wouldn't treat me right once the bloom was off the rose. It's time to walk away. I never enjoyed intimacy anyway."

"Things are really changing for women these days. We have so many more options now."

"Just like Helen Reddy's song. I love her."

"She's an inspiration for modern women. I play her records for motivation when I'm studying."

"I have her records, too. I play them to cheer myself up when I'm sad."

"We're both going to enjoy ourselves at the party, men or no men.

"You bet."

"I'd better get ready and warm up the Chicken A La King before Peter gets here."

"Have a nice time, Sandi."

"Thanks. See you later."

Arlene returned to her television. They were showing "I Dream Of Jeannie". The Valentine party was going to be the first time in over two weeks Steve and Olivia were going to come face to face. Though she was elated at the prospect of a budding relationship between them, she was filled with trepidation at the inevitable repercussions.

* * *

Steve's Uncle Lewis was at Mama Rosa's when I arrived. I smelled a setup but said nothing.

"Mrs. C., looking sharp!" Steve greeted me.

"Hello, dear."

Uncle Lewis was prompt in kissing my hand. I smiled uncomfortably. Enzo was playing "Isn't It Romantic?". I cringed. As Gayle and Mel walked in, I called out to them in desperation. They were prompt in assessing my circumstances and joined us.

A striking young woman with long black curls and warm brown eyes approached Steve. He put his arm around her shoulder.

"Mrs. C., I'd like you to meet my friend Shannon."

"Nice to meet you, Ma'am." she shook my hand politely; she had deep dimples.

"Nice to meet you, dear."

Gayle and Mel appeared to know her, as did Uncle Lewis. I did not know what impact this delightful creature was about to have on our Olivia. I hoped Gayle would enlighten me once we had a moment alone. Shannon was hugging Uncle Lewis and reminiscing about the late 1950's.

"This man saved my neck more times than I can count." she was laughing, her arm wound around his neck, "He signed all the notes my teachers sent home for my parents."

"She was always up to mischief, this one." he said, "A spitfire."

"I was always getting into fights."

"With the boys." Steve said.

"I didn't like being messed with. They pulled my hair, put bugs in my desk, tried to kiss me."

"So, you beat the crap out of them." Steve said, "You stood up for the kids who were too shy to stand up for themselves, too."

The song had changed to "Music To Watch Girls By".

"Will you excuse us?" Steve led Shannon to the dance floor.

I turned to Gayle sheepishly. She winked at me with a sly grin.

Sandi and Peter chose seats in a secluded corner. I scanned the restaurant for Arlene, however, could not see her. I excused myself to have a respite from the amorous glances Uncle Lewis was lavishing on me.

Steve and Shannon were laughing loudly as they danced.

"Do you remember the nasty cartoons of the teachers we used to draw?" she asked.

"You were racier than the rest of us. We only drew them in their underwear. You drew them naked." he laughed.

"I had such a crush on..."

"I know. You had so many crushes."

"I didn't tell a soul about them except you."

"You were worried your mom would find the torn-up pieces in the garbage."

"When we played school, you and I were drunk teachers dancing in the hallway. Poor Bryan played the flustered principal trying to control us. We sure had a lot of laughs, didn't we?"

"Sure did. Sometimes we laughed so hard, we peed ourselves. You were so much fun, I didn't think of you as a girl. Sorry."

"We were lucky kids, growing up in Sunshine Gardens."

"We were always in hot water. Bryan never got into trouble with Mom and Dad. I was the black sheep."

"Sharon was always the good girl. She loved snitching on me, too. At least, Bryan kept your secrets."

"It was all harmless stuff, though."

"Dick's parents didn't think so when I soaked him with the garden hose."

"He was asking for it. When you saw him bullying little Timmy, you lost your temper. I don't blame you. You were always a champion for the underdog."

"So were you, Steve. You still are."

"So are you. Teaching disabled kids takes a special kind of person."

"I want to hear more about this girl you're hooked on."

"Olivia. Olivia Cordova."

"Beautiful name. She must be very special."

"She is. There's no chance of it ever going anywhere, though."

"Hey, you're the biggest lady killer in town! Where's the old spirit?"

"She's out of my league."

"Don't be silly. There's no such thing."

"She's gorgeous, sophisticated, smart."

"What are you, chopped liver? No woman can resist that baby face...that blond hair, baby blue eyes..." she pinched his cheek, "Am I going to meet her?"

"She should be here soon."

"What's the story with this Kristy girl, anyway? You and I are pretending to be an item for her benefit, so she'll take the hint? Do you really think it's going to work?"

"I don't know, but I don't have any other ideas."

"It could backfire, but it could work, too. I'm in. I'll do anything for you."

I returned to find Uncle Lewis preparing to leave.

"I'm afraid this music's hard on the nerves." he said, "Good night, dear lady."

"Good night." I felt a twinge of guilt, "I hope you feel better."

"He's such a nice man, Mrs. C." Gayle said, "Why don't you give him a chance?"

"I'm too old, dear."

"You're never too old."

"I am, dear. For that. Believe me, I am."

Chapter 24/ Sacrifice

Arlene and Kristy arrived at the party, both of them appearing out of sorts. Arlene sat with us, however, did not speak. We did not press her. Hawkeye Kristy wasted no time spotting the laughing couple on the dance floor.

"Who's the slut hanging all over Steve?" she demanded to know.

"That's Shannon." Gayle stated.

"Shannon? Shannon's a girl?"

"You bet she is."

"And she's moving in with Steve?"

"Yup."

"I'll kill her!"

"Cool your jets, Kristy. He's a free agent."

"No he's not! He's mine! How did this slut get her hooks into him?"

"Rumor is, they've known each other for a very long time."

"He never mentioned her to me."

"Of course not." Mel winked.

"I'll kill her! I swear I'll kill her!"

"I'd be careful if I were you, saying those things in front of a police officer." Gayle said.

"You do know, don't you, Kristy," Mel smirked, "That Shannon's gay?"

Kristy's face was drained of all color. Perhaps for the very first time in her short life of twenty years, she was speechless. Gayle and Arlene led her toward the bar.

"I hope they keep her from getting too intoxicated." I said.

"That girl's a real piece of work." Mel shook his head.

"She thinks all women are competition." I said, "It must be such a terrible way to live."

"She's miserable, so she tries to make everyone else miserable, too."

Steve was still dancing with Shannon, totally oblivious to his surroundings.

"I'm dying to meet your Olivia." Shannon said, "Knowing you, I'd say she must be one sexy knockout."

"She's very special."

"You're really smitten. It's so cute." she pinched his cheek, "I hope she comes down soon. I promised Deirdre I'd get home in time to watch "Columbo" together."

"She'll be here soon. Nadya promised she'd get her here by hook or by crook."

"We should stop dancing, so she won't get the wrong idea." she pulled away, "Enjoy your new stereo, by the way. It was a clever touch in our scheme to make it look like I was moving in."

Shannon stopped talking, suddenly made aware and bemused by the sight of Steve's eyes transfixed on something behind her. She turned around to see precisely who she was expecting to find. She gasped.

Enzo changed the record to "At Last". In her splendor, Olivia floated in, sultry in a deep russet red dress, her glossy dark hair swinging freely past her shoulders, her frothy organza skirt swaying with her every step. An awe-struck Shannon took in every inch of her jaw-dropping luminescence. Olivia walked up to Steve and smiled.

"Would you like to dance?" she took his hand.

Shannon could feel the pounding of Steve's heart with Olivia so close to him. "At Last" was followed by "The More I See You".

"This song's one of my favorites." Olivia lifted her eyes to his face and kissed him.

His eyes widened and flickered. He pulled her into a long, tender kiss.

Olivia did not want the song to end. It felt so right to be in his arms, drinking in the light from his eyes. It had never felt "right" with the others. Dangerous, exciting, enticing, yes. But shallow and fleeting. With Steve, she felt sheltered by a sturdy oak.

They did not see the short circuit in Kristy's eyes, or the way she broke free from Gayle and Arlene and lunged at Olivia with a fork. Before she had the opportunity to strike, she was captured by Mel and Shannon. She kicked wildly and bit both of them on the hand. Vincent appeared promptly to help restrain her. Arlene and Gayle rushed to attempt to reason with Kristy, who was spewing off unintelligible profanities at Mel and Shannon.

"Get away from me, you freak!" she spat in Shannon's face, "Don't touch me! I know what you are!"

Shannon walked away, tears stinging her eyes. She was embraced by Joyce.

"You need to leave the premises, Kristy." Mel stated matter-of-factly, "You cannot stay here. I don't want to arrest you, but I'm warning you not to be on these premises or anywhere near Olivia."

"I'll take her over to my mom's." Arlene volunteered, "She's always up for company."

Steve was comforting Olivia. Enzo stopped the music. Nadya and Greg arrived at that moment and stood aside, perplexed. Arlene led Kristy out of the building. Mel announced:

"Everything's all right now, folks. Sorry for the disruption. Please return to the festivities."

Enzo put on Cat Stevens' "Wild World". Nadya joined Joyce and Sandi in comforting Shannon. Steve led Olivia to the seating area.

"I'm so sorry about this, Olivia." he held her hands in his.

"It's not your fault, Steve. Kristy's an unbalanced young woman."

"I won't let her harm a hair on your head. I'll keep you safe."

"If she weren't Arlene's cousin, I would've arrested her." Mel told them, "If she makes one wrong move, it's the end of the line. No more leniency. I'm sorry, Olivia."

"It's all right. You and that nice young girl prevented her from carrying out her plan. By the way, where is that girl? I'd like to thank her." she stood up and glanced around.

"There she is." Steve led her to Shannon, "Olivia, meet Shannon. She's one of my oldest friends."

"Thank you for doing what you did, Shannon." Olivia hugged her.

"Don't mention it. You're every bit as beautiful as Steve said you were."

"Thank you. Are you the Shannon who just moved in?"

"I didn't actually move in. Steve was getting a new stereo, so we staged it to look like I was his new roommate moving my stuff in. For Kristy's benefit. That psycho won't be coming around to bother you anymore."

"I'm sorry about what happened."

"Don't worry about it. I have to get going. My girlfriend must be wondering where I am. Have a lovely evening, folks."

"Thank you." Olivia hugged her again.

"It was very nice to meet you."

"Likewise. I wish it could've been under better circumstances."

"It's okay."

Shannon said her goodbyes to the others as Steve led Olivia to the lobby.

"I'll take you home if you like."

"Only if you stay with me." she took his hand, "Don't worry, I'm not drunk this time."

Back at the restaurant, Enzo was playing "My Funny Valentine". Sandi and Peter were having one final dance before he had to leave.

"I'm sorry the party was a flop." she said.

"Not at all. I enjoyed spending the evening with you. I hope we can see each other again."

"I would like that."

"I'll cook us dinner next time."

"I'll look forward to it."

Observing them from their seats, Joyce and Vincent smiled.

"The evening's salvageable, after all." he said.

"Those two are good for each other." she said.

"You want to see everyone happy. I love that about you."

"I wish little Shannon could be happy. Do you know that her parents disowned her when she came out to them? So did her sister. She has no family support."

"We're all a ragtag family of misfits in one way or another in this building. She would find a lot of support among us."

"She acts happy-go-lucky to hide her pain, but she's bleeding inside. Her girlfriend is not very supportive, either. It's an unequal relationship, with Shannon doing all the giving. Steve's been telling me about these things. He worries about her."

"Your maternal instinct is very strong."

"I'm so blessed to have you."

"So am I."

"They're playing "I've Grown Accustomed To Her Face". Do you want to dance?"

"I'd never pass up a chance to dance with my beautiful wife." he took her hand and led her to the dance floor.

They danced cheek to cheek, oblivious to the emptying restaurant and the dimming lights.

* * *

Intoxicated by her perfume as she led him up the stairs, his knees as wobbly as a young colt's, he followed her in trepidation. Her hand was silken inside his clammy palm. All of his dreams were coming true. He had waited so long for this moment, and feared it would never become reality. Yet, now, here she was, tantalizingly within his reach. He wished he were drunk. He wished both of them were. Once inside the apartment, she turned on the single-bulb frosted hallway light and stepped out of her uncomfortable shoes. He stood staring at her sheepishly. Tossing back her hair, she approached him with a sultry smile and traced the outline of his lips with a fingertip. He shuddered. Then, she drew him into a smoldering kiss. Feeling his desire for her, her agile fingers peeled away his jacket and tossed it across the room. She pulled away from him to loosen his tie and unbutton his shirt. Her tongue danced across his chest as her skillful fingers worked on his zipper. His shirt and tie flew across the room. His pants and briefs fell around his ankles. His hands shaking uncontrollably, he pulled down the straps of her dress. Fumbling around like an adolescent, he managed to find the zipper in the back of her dress and lowered it. She could see he was quivering with desire for her. She took both of his hands in hers and guided them where she wanted them. Her dress slid down, followed by her intimate wear. She pulled him down to the floor, wrapped her legs around his neck and took him in.

She was amazed by what a tender, unselfish lover he was, how he cared more about her pleasure than his own. She cuddled into him on the floor, and let her hand rest on his chest. She was moved and humbled by the way he treated her. She smiled tenderly at him. He kissed her softly and gazed upon her face with eyes so full of light that she fought back tears. No one had meant this much before. And no one ever would again.

* * *

"Hey, Pumpkin, what's wrong?" Nadya heard an unfamiliar man's voice in the hallway.

"Oh, Daddy, I don't like it here anymore."

"You haven't been here that long. Give it a chance, Pumpkin."

"Steve made it very clear he doesn't want to have a relationship with me."

"Give it time, dear. He needs a chance to get to know what a wonderful young lady you are."

"He's in love with an older woman."

"It's his loss, honey. You know you're welcome to move back home any time you want. I paid two months' rent ahead of time, so you're all fixed up until April if you decide to stay."

"I don't know, Dad."

"If you move out, what are you going to do with the furniture?"

"Sell it for twice as much as what you paid for it. It's outdated stuff, not to mention that light green is not anybody's favorite color, but it's really in good condition."

"The lady took good care of it."

Nadya stood before the kitchen sink, tears burning her eyes. Even someone as obnoxious as Kristy had a father who loved her. What was so flawed about her that she had not been deemed deserving of something that was taken for granted by little girls everywhere? Why had she been unable to experience having a father who gazed adoringly at her, called her his princess, and lifted her up in the air? Her father had expressed only contempt for her, from the beginning. She had been told daily she was nothing but an inconvenience, an annoyance and a financial burden. The two black holes that were her father's eyes haunted her in her nightmares, even today, those black holes which were passageways to his dark, soulless interior. His cold, mocking, smarmy smirk, his lecherous glances in her later years...All things dark and evil that her father embodied...

She wept uncontrollably, unable to muffle her sobs.

"What's that sound?" the man's voice was heard again, "Is somebody crying?"

"Ignore it, Dad. It's probably that cry-baby hippie chick."

"Something must be bothering her."

"Everything bothers her. Just ignore her. She's an attention-seeker."

"She's crying."

"She cries all the time. She probably got a paper cut or something. I'm the one with a crisis here: I've been rejected by the man I love. I want to move back home. The last thing I need is a constant reminder of him carrying on with another woman. How can I study for exams with those two flaunting their relationship in front of me?"

"Of course you can move back home, dear. You can get some of your stuff now and come home with me. I can send the movers to pack up the rest of your stuff and bring it later this week. You can put an ad in the newspaper for the furniture."

"Thanks, Daddy, I love you."

"I love you, too, Pumpkin."

* * *

Greg was going up the stairs when Arlene appeared, carrying a cardboard box.

"Arlene! What's going on?"

"I'm moving out." she said.

"Moving out?" he took the box from her, "What brought this on? I mean, besides Kristy getting evicted. Is that the reason?"

"Kristy needed to be evicted. There's no doubt about that. I think I need to leave, too. After all, I'm related to her."

"No one blames you for the way she turned out. You're not her keeper. You are loved here. No one wants you to leave."

"I need to be helping my aunt and uncle keep an eye on the problem child. They can't handle her by themselves."

"You're going to be missed. Nadya's going to be very upset. She's known you the longest, and values your friendship."

"I'm going to miss her, too. And everyone else, as well. But my family needs my help now."

"I'm sorry to hear that." he followed her outside.

"There are some pressing matters, as well. Kristy's pregnant."

"Not by Steve!"

"No. I think she was planning to trick Steve into thinking it was his, but he refused to sleep with her. Very wise of him. Her pregnancy is the result of a short relationship she had with a South American student."

"Steve had a lucky escape."

"My aunt, Cousin Doreen and I have to take Kristy down to Maine for an abortion before her exams."

"Whoa! She's a real handful!"

"You can say that again."

They were in the parking lot, where a scowling middle-aged man with a baseball cap was waiting by a rusty old pick-up truck, whom she introduced as Leroy.

Leroy's handshake was limp and weak. He also seemed to have misplaced his vocal chords. Greg loaded the box into Leroy's truck.

"Thank you for carrying my box, Greg." Arlene climbed into the truck beside Leroy, "I'll be back tomorrow for the rest of my stuff and to clean up. I'll come later in the day, so I can catch Nadya. Give her my love."

"I will. Take care."

Leroy started the noisy engine and sped away, tires squealing. Shaking his head in disbelief, Greg returned to the building.

Chapter 25/ Love Is All

Joyce's fingertip caressed the face in the framed black and white photograph. The haunting dark eyes of the teen looked back at her. Her chin-length dark hair was pulled away from her face with a scarf tied as a hairband. She was wearing a plaid shirt-waist dress with cuffed puffy sleeves.

..."That son of a bitch took everything away from Lena...The light in her eyes went out. Her life was over the moment he touched her..." she remembered the day Vincent had shared his painful past with her, "My sister became addicted to heroin and committed suicide. I couldn't protect her from him. I failed her."

"You did not fail her. You couldn't prevent your father from doing what he did. You were just a teen yourself. There was nothing you could've done to produce a different outcome. Vincent, you loved her and you did everything in your power to protect her. Lena would never blame you for anything."

"I reported him and made sure he would never be able to get near her again. He went to prison, and he was killed by an inmate. My mother never forgave me for leaving her without him."

"She was wrong to do that."

"Mother was a Manic Depressive. I tried my best to take care of her to the very end. She blamed me for the way things turned out and resented me for doing well for myself."

"I'm so sorry you had to go through so much pain."

"My sister was the only innocent, the only real victim. She never deserved any of the things that happened to her. That bastard destroyed her. He got what he deserved in prison. Mother failed to protect Lena from that monster, because she cared only about her own selfish needs. They made Lena a sacrificial lamb. She never had a chance, with those vultures as parents."

"But she had you."

"I was useless."

"No. She knew you loved her. There was nothing else humanly possible you could've done. Vincent, please forgive yourself..."...

Joyce kissed the photo and placed it back on the shelf.

* * *

A cold rain was beating down on the winter-weary streets. Snowbanks of butterscotch ripple ice-cream were melting into rivulets of dishwater along the edges of the sidewalks. The ominous grey of the sky threatened to bestow more of its wrath upon us.

Nadya pulled her bulky grey cardigan tighter around herself. Greg came up behind her and wrapped his arms around her. She stroked his hand. He feared for her when she retreated into that dark place she had not been able to obliterate. The scorch marks of her past remained seared on her soul.

News of her pregnancy must have reached those busybodies' ears by now. Someone must have caught a glimpse of the two of them buying maternity and baby items. The silent treatment from her parents nagged at him. It was out of character for that duo to back off without drama. He kept his suspicions to himself, for he was aware that a small part of her would still miss them. Despite their unrelenting torture, and undeniable malice toward her, the meticulously measured small gestures of kindness had been successful brainwashing tools. Nadya had remained loyal and obliging to the point of jeopardizing her own mental and physical health. He was grateful to Vincent and Joyce for helping him understand Stockholm Syndrome. Nadya herself was working diligently to come to terms with the traces of affection that continued to co-exist alongside the fear, repulsion and contempt her oppressors inspired. He longed to protect her from their callous narcissism.

She turned around and gazed up at him with those innocent eyes. He kissed her forehead and pulled her close. She caressed his smooth cheek. He kissed the small white hand he loved dearly. She planted soft kisses on his nose, eyebrows, cheeks and lips. He pressed her against the wall and kissed her. She wrapped one leg around him. He pulled her dress up to her neck and buried his face in her breasts. She moaned in longing. He turned her around and entered her from behind. She pressed her palms against the wall. With every scream, she slammed her palms against the wall. When he pulled her back into his arms, she kept her face buried in his chest.

"I'll get you a facecloth." He released her.

She did not want to erase any part of him from her body. He returned and insisted on doing the job himself, kneeling in front of her, moving the cloth in soft caresses as he washed off his own deposit. She wanted him to overpower her again, and breathe life into her corpse-like body...make her feel she belonged in the world. He patted her small bulge and placed his face against it.

"Hey, little one, this is your daddy." he crossed his eyes, stuck out his tongue, and made faces, "Your daddy's a big clown. You and Mommy mean the world to me. I'm going to take care of you and keep you safe."

"This baby's very lucky to have you for a daddy."

"And to have you for a mommy. Baby Nadya's going to be one spoiled daddy's girl."

"We can't name the baby Nadya."

"Why not? It's the most beautiful name I've ever heard. And unique."

"Too unique. I didn't like standing out from the crowd at school. No one could pronounce it. They asked a million questions."

"You just wait. In another ten years or so, it's going to be a super popular name."

"I don't know about that."

"You said, if it's a boy, we'll name him Greg. Why can't we name her Nadya if she's a girl?" he quirked his eyebrows.

"How about a compromise, then?"

"I'm all for that."

"Why don't we call her Nadine? It's the French version of my name and has the same meaning and origin."

"You've got it." he patted her again, pulled up her panties, and lowered her dress.

"Just think," he returned to the bathroom to clean up, "In another month, the Cape Cod on Reid Street is going to be on the market. Eleanor says we have first dibs on it and it's in move-in condition...Close to schools, close to the university, within walking distance of both uptown and downtown."

"We're going to have the idyllic life we've dreamed about."

"Life is idyllic for me no matter where we are, as long as we're together." he returned to the room, "I have to get us some groceries before Eat-Rite closes."

"Why don't we go together?"

He helped her put on her coat and zipped up her boots. He thought about her being a new mother without the support of an extended family and wished he could make life better for her.

"I hope Baby Greg'll be strong and loving like you."

"I hope Baby Nadine'll be gentle and captivating like you." he took her arm and guided her down the stairs.

The rain had stopped. The air was fragrant with the scent of moist earth. Emerging from the red brick supermarket was Gwen, wearing one of her trademark stretch polyester teal green pants and a beige bomber jacket that cut her off at the waist and emphasized her enormous bottom.

"Hello, Greg." she burst into her saccharine smile, "Looking handsome as ever."

Greg squeezed Nadya's arm and quickened his steps.

"A gorgeous man like you shouldn't be saddled with a family." Gwen continued, "Any time you need a break from the drudgery, you know you can call on me."

Her permanently etched smug look was too nauseating for him to see. She was balancing a brown leather shoulder bag and three paper bags of groceries.

"Just ignore her." he whispered to Nadya.

"Just keep walking, Gwen." he said, "There's nothing for you here."

"You'll be singing a different tune when the baby keeps you awake every night crying."

"Hit the road, Gwen." he pulled Nadya away.

Nadya glanced over to observe Gwen from the back as she walked toward the parking lot. Under the glaring lights outside the supermarket, the cube shape of the woman's buttocks astonished her. She wondered what type of foundation garment or alternate contraption had caused it and why she would have wanted to achieve that particular look in the first place.

"She's got a cube bum." she whispered.

"She's got a what???" his eyes widened.

"Her bum is shaped like a cube!"

He burst out laughing and drew her into a tight embrace.

"How did I ever live before I met you?"

They stood outside Eat-Rite, holding on to one another, oblivious to the station wagon coasting by, with sinister eyes glaring from the darkened interior.

* * *

Joyce opened the door when she recognized Vincent's footsteps in the hallway. Dry cleaning bags were slung over his shoulder while he carried his briefcase. She took the dry cleaning from him and hung them up from the hall rack.

"I have some other stuff in the car." he said, placing his briefcase on the floor.

"I'll come down and help."

"No, no. These are too heavy. I'll make two trips."

"I'm intrigued. What did you buy?"

"You'll see." he ran down the hall.

She smiled and stood in the doorway.

"Hi, Joyce." Steve was coming out of her former apartment, "Everything okay?"

"Vince went back down to the car to get something special he bought, but he wouldn't tell me what it was, except that there were more than one and they were heavy."

"I'll go down and give him a hand."

"Thank you. That's very nice of you."

"No problem."

It was always a blessing to see the sun shining out of Vincent's languid eyes on these occasions; she had only seen clouds for so long. The two men returned, each cradling a cardboard box.

"What in the world are those?" she asked.

"Fireproof safes. One for your thesis and one for mine."

"Wow." she shook her head in disbelief, "You think of everything, honey."

"You can store any valuable documents, photos, mementos. Everyone should have one."

"Let's spread the word." Steve said, "By the way, Joyce, I'm moving into your old apartment."

"Closer to Olivia." Vince winked.

"Sarge didn't want a vacant apartment or a new tenant on this floor. He's already lined up a journalist lady for my old apartment and an engineering student for that Fred guy's apartment for April."

"That's great news, Steve." Joyce said.

"I'm glad Sarge moved Mrs. C. into Arlene's old apartment. It's good to have her close by. Well, I'd better get going." Steve said.

"Thanks for lending me a hand, buddy." Vincent patted his back.

"Any time. See you guys later."

Joyce embraced Vincent.

"You're full of surprises, honey."

"I thought there had to be a better way than keeping them in the freezer, so I looked into it. We can also keep our wedding photos and homemade tapes in them."

"It's very prudent. Thank you."

"I'm glad it pleases you." he smiled, "Are we still on for looking at more houses this Sunday?"

"You bet we are."

"We'll find the perfect brick bungalow of your dreams one of these days." he hung up his coat in the closet, "I'll get the safes all set up right now." he said with the excitement of a young child.

"Not yet. Please let me just stay in your arms a bit longer." Joyce pleaded.

He smelled clean and pure like a mountain spring. She craved the soothing warmth of his body. He kissed her cheek, squishing his soft nose into her skin. She started nibbling on his nose.

"Mmm...That feels good."

"I don't want to give you a hickey." she pulled away.

"You can do anything you want to me. I'm your love slave. Have your wicked way with me."

She longed to shelter him from the clamor of the world, soothe the well of dried tears in his soul, make him an innocent child again, untouched by the dark. She took his hand and led him into the bedroom. She sat on the edge of the bed and pulled her dress up over her head. He fell to his knees in front of her. His long, delicate fingers caressed her thighs, lingered on her sacred place, sending her into spasms. She nudged him on to the bed and slid under him.

Lying in his arms in the afterglow, she wished time would stay still like this for eternity. Her tears fell on his chest. He kissed her forehead. She lifted her eyes to his face and saw the tears shining in his eyes. With her fingertip, she traced a heart on his lips. They remained there long after the final fingers of sunset had gone to sleep.

* * *

"What's this?" Olivia asked as Steve brought in a box wrapped in green paper.

"A Saint Patrick's Day present."

"I didn't know people exchanged presents on Saint Patrick's Day."

"I'm starting a new trend."

"You're full of surprises."

"This is something practical. Come on. Open it."

Olivia removed the wrapping paper and stared blankly at the cardboard box.

"It looks like a strong box. What is it for?"

"Your thesis and other important stuff. It's a fireproof safe."

"Wow."

"I thought you could use it."

"Thank you, Steve. It's very thoughtful of you." she kissed his cheek, "It must've cost a fortune."

"Vince bought a couple of them for him and Joyce. That's when I decided to get one for you. Greg got a couple of them; Sandi got one. Everyone's jumping on the bandwagon."

"I hope you got one for yourself."

"All my stuff is at my parents' house. I just have clothes and records here. My stereo's the most valuable thing I own and it wouldn't fit into one of these."

"What did I ever do to deserve you?" she gazed at him tenderly, "Steven Henderson, you are the most terrific guy I've ever known."

"I'm the luckiest guy in the world."

"Steve, you've made me happier than anyone I've ever known. I want to be with you for as long as you'll have me."

"Olivia, you're all I've ever dreamed of."

He was still that shy, youthful boy she had taken to bed for the first time on Valentine's Day. His fingers fumbled with her dress tentatively. He still needed to be convinced she wanted him, too. Her caresses made him moan. He surrendered to her skillful touch, letting her undress him slowly. Her hands danced playfully. She wanted to hear his cries of ecstasy. She wanted him to know he was cherished the way he made her feel at peace and secure in the knowledge that she was loved.

* * *

The Saint Patrick's Day party downstairs was rowdy, as we had all expected. Alcohol was flowing freely, Irish songs were being sung off-key, and laughter reached its highest decibels. Greg was dancing with Vincent, Mel, Steve and Peter, while singing louder than everyone else in the restaurant. All the men wore green ties. I sat in the corner with the rest of the ladies, nibbling on shamrock shaped sugar cookies covered in green sprinkles, drinking pistachio ice cream and club soda floats. There was also a green cake with green frosting, decorated with green maraschino cherries. Olivia was the only one who ordered an alcoholic beverage: A grasshopper, but stopped after one drink and ordered a float like the rest of us. She was striking as always in her green sequined party dress. Each one of us had made an effort to wear at least one green item of clothing. Sandi's was a hunter green plaid skirt she wore with a grey turtleneck. Joyce was classy in an emerald green jersey dress. Nadya was dressed in floor length maternity wear in a moss green paisley print. Gayle was the bold one in her slinky, low-cut lime green gown. I had only a silk scarf in a green geometric print, tied around my neck as a kerchief.

Vincent and Peter joined us while the remaining men continued the merriment with their arms around each other.

"Tomorrow's Monday. I think I'd best be going." Peter said.

"I think I'd better get forty winks myself. Good night, folks. See you tomorrow." Sandi walked out to the lobby with him.

"Well, dear, this old guy is all tuckered out." Vincent said.

Her eyes overflowing with love, Joyce took his arm.

"Good night, folks." they spoke in unison on their way out.

"I wish Arlene could've been here, too." Nadya said, "I miss hearing her Dolly Parton records when I walk by that door."

"We all miss her, too." Olivia closed her hand over hers.

"Here come the boys." Gayle remarked, "They look wasted."

Mel pulled Gayle to her feet and attempted to dance with her.

"I think you've done enough dancing for the night, dear." she patted his head and led him away.

Greg took Nadya's arm, however, she was the one who had to steady him. Steve hooked one arm through Olivia's and the other through mine. On the stairs, all three of us were tripping over each other and laughing like children. At that moment of innocence, we permitted ourselves to believe that no one could shatter our fairy tale existence.

Chapter 26/ Don't Say Goodbye

March the 19th, 1974 began as an ordinary day. Gayle and Mel drove off to work together before dawn. George and Ethel packed their black Parisienne for their weekly trip to Gagetown to visit George's elderly mother as they did every Tuesday like clockwork. Joyce, Sandi and Olivia walked down the stairs together, engaged in conversation.

"Stop worrying. You've got him all set up with chicken soup, chicken salad sandwiches and a garden salad, Vick's Vapo Rub and Kleenex on the bed stand." Sandi said.

"You love pampering him, don't you?" Olivia said.

"I wish I could've gotten out of this meeting with Dr. Black, so I could've stayed home to take care of him, but she wouldn't hear of it. She demanded that I meet with her." Joyce's voice could be heard.

"He'll be all right." Sandi said.

"I hate leaving him alone when he's sick."

"Don't worry." Olivia said.

From my window, I observed the trio in trench coats as they rounded the corner of the building: Joyce's coat in pebble white, Olivia's in scarlet red, and Sandi's in navy blue.

"Why don't we just go in my car?" Sandi suggested, "We're all going to the same place. And, if you want to leave early, Joyce, we can use it as an excuse to do the same. It's a long day of research at the law library for me, so I can leave any time."

"I'm in." Olivia said.

"Me, too." Joyce agreed.

"Carpooling's good for the environment, too." Sandi reminded them jovially.

I was hurrying to prepare for my dentist appointment. I put on my wool-lined grey trench coat, though it was mild enough for my unlined one on that day. I wanted to keep warm to avoid the flu that was sweeping through the building. Nadya and Greg were home with the same symptoms as Vincent's. As I locked my door, I saw Steve coming up the stairs, carrying an Eat-Rite bag.

"Hey, Mrs. C. Looking sharp." he greeted me.

"I'm on my way to the dentist. Root canal."

"Good luck, Mrs. C. I was going to ask you to share these pastries with me, but it looks like we'll have to do it another time. Maybe tomorrow. I work nights all this week, so I'm home during the day."

"That would be very nice, dear."

"I'll save you some from this batch. Maybe you can have a midnight snack after the freezing comes off."

"You're a sweetheart." I pinched his youthful cheek.

"I'll see you later, Mrs. C. Let me know if there's anything you need."

"Thanks, dear. Enjoy your day."

I walked the seven blocks to my dentist's office. The waiting room of the converted Victorian house was full. I glanced around uneasily.

"We're ready for you, Mrs. Carleton." the grey-haired receptionist addressed me in her usual businesslike manner.

"It smells like fresh paint." I attempted to make small talk as she prepared me for the procedure, "The cream color looks lovely."

"You should've seen it last week. The young fellows he hired to paint it on the weekend before went to town and painted it pink and purple. When we all got here on that Monday, our jaws dropped. So, he got them to come back and repaint it this past weekend." she shook her head, "Hippies. What else can you expect?"

"It just sparkles now." I said.

"Good morning, Blanche." My dentist came in, "How are things?"

"Pretty good, doctor."

"I'm going to freeze you now, okay?"

I closed my eyes and dug my nails into my palms.

* * *

Enzo pushed open the back door of the restaurant, descended the stairs, and deposited a trash bag into the dumpster. Leaning against the iron railing of the back stairs, he lit up a cigarette. Gazing at the steel grey river, and the heavily wooded North side of Elmdale across it, he inhaled deeply. Two white vans drove into the parking lot and parked along the outer edge of the lot. Across their sides, "Ace Flooring" was printed in red letters. Two men in grey coveralls came out of one of the vans, opened the back, removed a rolled up carpet and headed toward the building. Two men in identical garb in the other van proceeded to do the same. Someone held the back door to the apartments open for them. Enzo's view of that door was partially obstructed by the dumpster. It appeared renovations were underway for the apartments.

"Enzo! Enzo! Where is that boy?" his father's voice was heard from inside the restaurant.

Enzo threw his cigarette on the ground and stepped on it to extinguish it. Sighing, he returned to the restaurant kitchen to find his father frantically waving his arms. His fleshy face was flushed; the nostrils of his meaty nose were flaring, with hairs protruding from them. The fabric of his white shirt was stretched to its limit across his protruding abdomen. Enzo feared he might look the same way at that age. His dreams and plans did not include running the family restaurant into old age. Remaining in this backwoods small town was not an acceptable option. For now, he would live out his days as deejay for the restaurant, and dream of his big break in the music industry.

* * *

Footsteps could be heard coming up the back stairs. Vincent was in the kitchen, pouring himself coffee. Uneasy about this activity, he dialed Greg and Nadya's number.

"Greg, some people are coming up the back stairs. That door does not open from outside. Someone from the building had to have let them in."

“There’ve been some burglaries in this area lately.” Greg said, “I thought it was odd when the phone rang a little while ago and no one was there. I’ll take care of it, buddy. Thanks for letting me know, Vince. Stay inside your apartment and lock your door.”

Vincent attempted to call 911 after hanging up, however, discovered the phone lines had been cut within that split second.

Nadya threw her arms around Greg’s neck.

“Honey, please don’t go out there.”

“There might be burglars in the building, sweetheart.” Greg put on his holster and retrieved his service revolver from the filing cabinet; he placed his badge in the back pocket of his jeans, “Stay here and keep the door locked. I’ll check it out.”

“Be careful.” she kissed him.

Greg emerged from their apartment and locked the door behind him. Down the hall, Steve appeared.

“Hold it right there! What are you doing?” Greg demanded of the strangers who descended on them.

“Putting down new carpets.”

“None of us have heard anything about new carpets being installed in the building.”

“The owner doesn’t need permission from the tenants.”

“Who let you in?” Greg demanded.

“The landlord.” the thinnest intruder retorted, dropping his carpet.

“I don’t think so.” Steve said, flashing his badge, “Hold it right there. Police. Don’t move.”

Both Greg and Steve had their guns on the intruders. The thin man and his tallest accomplice put their hands up. The other two resisted. Another man came up the stairs and fired at Steve from the back. He fell, bleeding from his head. Greg fired a shot and wounded the gunman in the chest. The thin man fired at Greg. He fell. Behind him, the apartment door opened and another gunman dragged a hysterical Nadya out to the hallway, his gun pointed at her head.

"Caught this one climbing down the fire escape."

"Shoot her. What're you waiting for?"

Another shot rang out and she fell on top of Greg. Vincent's door opened and another gunman appeared, pointing his gun at Vincent's head.

"Lookee here, boys. Big guy tried to sneak down the fire escape to get help for his buddies. Ain't that nice?"

Another shot, and Vincent fell, lifeless, with a loud thud. The gunmen wrapped carpets around Nadya and Greg. Four of them carried them out to the back. Two others followed them and swiftly returned with two more carpets. Vincent was wrapped in the third one and carried out by two men. As the lone remaining gunman approached Steve with the last carpet, he heard footsteps coming up the stairs.

I was returning home, holding on to the railing and pausing at each step, still groggy from my ordeal at the dentist's office. As I reached the top of the stairs, someone fired at me. Another gunman returned to help him.

"Let's get the fuck outta here!"

"What about these two?"

"There's no time. Leave them. No one can tie them to us. Come on. Let's get the fuck out before anyone else comes back and we have to kill them, too."

Downstairs, the lunch crowd at Mama Rosa's was laughing and listening to the Italian songs Enzo was playing.

"What was all that noise?" Mama Rosa whispered to Enzo.

"I think there's a car or a truck backfiring, Mama."

"I heard some other noises, too, like someone moving furniture."

"There are workers upstairs doing renovations."

"I hope they're done before the supper crowd gets here."

"These folks haven't noticed anything, Mama. They're having too good a time, drinking wine and listening to music. The supper crowd's going to be drinking even more. Don't worry about it, Ma."

Upstairs, Steve and I lay lifeless on the stained avocado carpet in the hallway that reeked of cigarette smoke from decades of former tenants. Two of the gunmen returned with cans of gasoline. They doused me and Steve first, and went through the building. Then, they tossed a lit match and scuttled away like rats before The Splendid exploded in flames that lit up the skies of Elmdale.

Chapter 27/ Softly As I Leave You

"Are you two ladies ready to blow this Popsicle stand?" Sandi stood outside Joyce's office door.

"We were just on our way to get you." Joyce was gathering her papers and placing them in her briefcase.

Olivia was standing on the other side of Joyce's desk. Joyce put on her coat, followed them out and locked the door behind her. Olivia pressed the elevator button across the hall.

"There must be a big fire somewhere downtown." Sandi said as they entered the elevator and she pressed the button for the lobby, "When I came out of Ludlow Hall, I could see flames shooting up in the sky. It looks bad."

"Oh, dear." Joyce shuddered.

Olivia placed an arm around her. As they stepped off the elevator, they found Peter, Mel, and John Silverman, Mel's partner, waiting in the lobby.

"What are you guys doing here?" Olivia asked.

"We were just on our way up to find you." John said; he was a tall, grey-haired man with amber-tinted glasses.

"What's wrong?" Joyce's voice quivered.

"I wish you could all sit down before we tell you." Mel said, glancing around the barren lobby which offered no seating.

"Go on. Tell us." Sandi urged him.

"The Splendid's on fire." Mel stated hoarsely, "She's going fast. Spreading like crazy. Three whole blocks of Queen from Westmorland to Regent are on fire."

Joyce's face faded to a bluish white, and she fell, unconscious, on the terrazzo floor. Peter, Mel and John gathered her up. Peter cradled her in his arms. Olivia picked up Joyce's purse and slung it on her shoulder with her own. She also picked up her briefcase and tucked it under her arm.

"I'll take her to my car." Peter said, "We can all meet up at my house."

Mel and John held the heavy doors of Keirstead Hall open for him. Olivia and Sandi solemnly followed Peter outside.

"I think you two ought to go with Peter, as well." John said.

"My car's here." Sandi told him.

"I'll drive your car there." Mel offered, holding out his hand for her keys.

"I'm parked behind the library, not in my usual parking spot. I drove up from Ludlow Hall to pick up Joyce and Liv."

"I'll follow in the squad car." John said.

Peter placed Joyce in the backseat. Olivia placed their purses and briefcases on the floor and sat beside her, propping her head on her lap. Sandi sat up front.

"Peter, did everyone get out okay?" Olivia asked.

"I'm not sure, Liv. Mel and John can tell us more when we get to the house."

None of them spoke during the short drive to Peter's blond-brick bungalow. He held the car doors open for all three of them. Joyce stumbled out, with Peter and Sandi each taking one of her arms and leading her up the concrete walkway. Olivia carried the handbags and briefcases. Peter unlocked the front door and led them into the living room, where he placed his sister on the sofa.

"I'll get her some ice." Sandi volunteered.

Mel and John arrived as Sandi was placing a bag of frozen peas on Joyce's forehead.

"Mel, did everyone get out okay?" Olivia asked.

"It's not good, I'm afraid, Liv. No one from your floor is accounted for. All we know for certain is, Mama Rosa's was evacuated immediately without incident, and no one was home on the second floor. The fire is still too intense for even the firemen to go inside."

"Vincent! Where's Vincent?" Joyce cried out.

"What about Steve?" Olivia asked.

"I'm sorry. No one's seen them, or Greg, Nadya, or Mrs. C."

"No!" Joyce burst into tears.

She and Olivia held on to one another.

"Enzo said there were some workers doing renovations in the building. I know Dad never mentioned anything about renovations or authorized any workers to come in. Enzo noticed two white vans with Ace Flooring on them in red lettering. Someone let the workers in through the back door. We're treating this as arson and conducting a criminal investigation."

"I've got to go and look for Vince." Joyce attempted to get up.

"Joyce, you can't!" Olivia held her shoulders.

"I can't just sit here and do nothing when he's missing."

"The entire police force is out looking for him."

"They already have their hands full. Let me help look for him."

"Oh, sweetheart." Olivia embraced her.

"I'll go look." Sandi said, "Let me see what I can do, Joyce. You need to stay here with Liv. I'll go, ask around, and see what I can dig up. Someone must have noticed something."

"I'm going with you." Peter stated.

"All right, but you two are not going on your own." Mel said, "Lesley Anne is going to accompany you. Come to the station and she'll meet you."

Sandi embraced Joyce and stroked her back.

"I'm going to do everything humanly possible to make things right for you." she held her face in her hands, "I'll call and check in with you two." she kissed Joyce's forehead.

"We'll be fine, Sandi." Olivia reassured her.

"Hang in there, Joycie." Peter stroked her hair and kissed the top of her head.

"Let's go in your car, Pete." Sandi said, handing her own car keys to Olivia, "Just in case you need to go anywhere."

Olivia nodded and gave her a knowing glance.

"On the way back, we'll pick up some basic necessities."

"I'll move into the den." Peter said, "Joycie, the master bedroom is yours. And, you two ladies decide between yourselves which one of the other two bedrooms you want."

"I'm sorry to put you out, Pete." Joyce said.

"Don't worry about it. This is the least I can do."

"Let's get going." Sandi said, "We'll check in with you."

"Thank you, guys." Olivia said.

"Be safe out there." Joyce said, with a hand on Olivia's arm.

* * *

"Your neighbors are going to think you're starting your own harem." Sandi slid two fried eggs on to a plate and placed it on the table in front of Peter, "Not only are Liv and I living here, but Arlene and Shannon are spending so much time visiting us."

"You all need each other for moral support. I appreciate the way your friends are standing by you at your time of need. I know Joyce does. She's still quite shaky."

"I can hear her crying in her sleep. She's having nightmares." she slid the remaining egg on to her own plate and sat beside him at the table.

"I'm worried about her, Sandi."

"So am I. She's always been the strong one for all of us at The Splendid. This shook her right to the core."

"She may never be all right again." Peter said.

"I'm dreading the identification of the two casualties they found." Sandi said, "When they get the dental records, if one turns out to be Vincent, I don't even want to think what it could do to her."

"I hope they get the sons of bitches who did this."

"I have a pretty good idea who those sons of bitches are. So does Mel."

"Sandi," he reached for her hand, "We'll get through this together."

She patted his hand.

"You're trying to be strong for Joyce and Olivia, but you've got to give yourself a break, allow yourself to grieve, to be human." he placed an arm around her shoulder.

They heard gentle footsteps coming down the hall. A pale Joyce with dark circles under her eyes was wrapped in an oversized fuzzy pink robe, a gift from Arlene, appearing even more delicate. She smiled weakly.

"Hi, sweetheart." Sandi went to hug her and noticed how frail she felt, "Have a seat. I'll get you some coffee."

"Hey, sis." Peter helped her to a seat at the table.

Sandi poured her a mug of coffee from the percolator, added cream and sugar, and stirred it before placing it in front of her.

"Thank you, Sandi. You really don't have to do all this for me. I need to start pulling my own weight around here."

"I want to do it. How about some eggs?"

"Please don't go to any trouble. I'm not hungry."

"You have to eat, so you can keep up your strength."

"I'll just have toast and marmalade, but I'll get it myself."

"No. Sit." Sandi ordered her, proceeding to place bread in the toaster.

"Pete, you're late for work. You don't have to change your routines because of me."

"I'm taking more time off." he patted her hand.

"Since Arlene doesn't work Mondays, she picked up Liv for some shopping. They're buying clothes for the three of us. They said we can pay them later." Sandi told her, "Shannon's coming over after work with a couple of casseroles."

"I'm so grateful to all of you. I don't know where I'd be without you."

"You never have to find out."

"Thank you."

"Those safes held up well through the inferno." Peter said, "The contents all survived."

"Thank God."

"They're all in the basement, all cleaned up. Mel brought them all here."

"Yours, Vince's, Liv's, mine, Nadya's and Greg's."

"Some good news for a change." Joyce smiled, picking at her toast, "How is everyone else making out? I hope they're all right."

"You don't have to take on the problems of the world on your shoulders." Sandi said, "Mel and Gayle have been living in the basement apartment of his parents' house in Skyline Acres. George retired. He and Ethel moved to Gagetown to be close to family. The Romanos are moving to Toronto. Mama Rosa has family there. Everyone's just fine."

"I should go and see it."

"No, Joyce. You don't want to do that."

"They haven't identified the two victims they found in the rubble yet, have they?"

"They're waiting for all the dental records. Joyce, please, don't torture yourself like this."

As long as Vince was not identified as one of the victims, Sandi thought, there was still a glimmer of hope. As long as he was missing, there was a possibility he might be alive and unable to contact any of them. She prayed they did not have to face the finality of an identification, for she knew Joyce would not survive that.

Chapter 28/ The Bridge

Steve and I were not discovered for a week. That is how long it took to put out that fire. Two blocks of the business district were reduced to rubble. We were burnt beyond recognition. Queen Street had the surreal appearance of a war-torn science fiction alternate universe. The fire jumped from one tinderbox to another on both sides of the street, travelling along power lines, setting off one explosion after another. The smell of death and destruction hung heavy in the air.

The five of us kept vigil at Peter's house. Vincent never left Joyce's side, and Steve, Olivia's. We remained together until Nadya, Greg, and Steve needed to cross over. Vincent remained as long as he possibly could, however, was whisked off against his will. Then, it was only me.

My nieces gave me a tasteful send-off. As a fallen officer, Steve received a ceremony befitting the hero he had been. Nadya, Greg, and Vincent were reported missing. A reward was offered for information leading to their whereabouts. Deep down, everyone was certain they were no longer among the living.

The fire was ruled as arson. Every possible lead was followed and ended in futility. Enzo came forward with his account of the "Ace Flooring" vans, however, no such company and no such vans were ever in existence. None of the amateur sleuths formerly hired to follow Nadya were proven to have ties to this crime.

Mel Elliott and Gayle Johnson, who had been the closest to Greg, were unable to deal with their grief. Once the investigation hit a dead end, they moved to Vancouver where they found folks were more tolerant of interracial unions.

No one was able to trace the whereabouts of Fred, the mystery tenant, or his associate Iggy.

Arlene Simmons remained with her aging mother. She was able to open her own beauty shop. Over the years, she fell out of touch with the others.

Joyce Greenfield completed her PhD. In Psychology and secured a teaching position at the university.

Olivia Cordova also completed her PhD. In Psychology and opened a private practice as a Child Psychologist.

Sandra Ames completed law school and became a passionate crown prosecutor, fiercely dedicated to seeking justice for victims of violent crimes.

The businesses destroyed on that day were rebuilt. Shiny new brick concealed the evil that had once visited us. The corner where our "Splendid" had once stood remained empty, neglected, overgrown with weeds, and decorated with political signs before every election. Joyce, Sandi and Olivia placed fresh flowers there every year on the anniversary of our deaths.

Boris and Ana garnered much sympathy from the community, posing as grief-stricken parents. Within two years, Ana lost her battle with cancer. Boris sat with her for hours each day to the very end. No glue is as strong as the one that binds partners in crime. Boris wasted no time in replacing her with a much younger partner in crime.

Then, one day, there it was: A new bridge was to be built, connecting that corner with the northern communities across the river. The undeveloped land behind the empty lot, where few had ventured before, was to be filled in and a new street was to be developed by the river to accommodate the elaborate network of roundabouts for the new bridge. Elmdale would never be the same again.

Chapter 29/ Eternal Cycle

"This is Michelle with your seven o'clock news." the radio came on, "The human remains discovered at the excavation site for the new bridge have been identified as: Nadezhda Olga Logan, 39, Gregory John Logan, 44, and Vincent Robert Greenfield, 47. Nadezhda Logan was four months pregnant at the time of her death. The victims were residents of Splendid Hotel, where the bodies of Blanche Edna Carleton, 67, and Steven Keith Henderson, 26 were found immediately following the fire in 1974. Their deaths were ruled as foul play. No arrests have been made to date. Police urge anyone with information to come forward. We'll keep you up to date on new developments...Today's weather: Sunny with cloudy periods..." the radio was shut off.

* * *

The children clutched their mother's hands as the casket was lowered into the ground. Their fearful eyes scanned the faces of the people in the crowd. Young Vinnie, in his dark suit, with his father's dark eyes, curly brown hair and soft upturned nose surveyed his surroundings with a furrowed brow. Little Beverly in her black velvet dress and with her blonde ponytail fastened at the nape of her neck, had her mother's translucent skin and blue eyes. She drew closer to her mother. A pale, gaunt Joyce held on to the children, her tear-streaked face concealed by the veil of her black fascinator. Her long-sleeved black dress hung loosely on her, giving her the appearance of a child wearing her mother's clothing. She pressed the children to her chest. The wind through the branches of the maple trees was whispering: "I'm always with you. I'll never leave you."

Sandi and Lesley Anne were huddled together away from others, whispering with solemn faces as the crowd began dispersing.

It was following my funeral six years earlier that Joyce learned she was pregnant. When she collapsed on her way to Peter's car and all attempts to revive her were unsuccessful, Peter, Sandi and Olivia transported her to the hospital. Following a comprehensive set of tests, she was given the news.

"Pregnant? I can't be. I'm forty-six years old. I thought I was going into menopause."

"You're eight weeks pregnant, Mrs. Greenfield. There's no doubt about it."

Learning that she was carrying twins was an even bigger surprise. I wished Vincent had not been called away to cross over before learning he was going to be a father. Beverly Nadine Bianca and Vincent Gregory Todd were welcomed on October 29th, 1974 by their doting mother, devoted Uncle Peter and an adoring group of honorary aunts.

* * *

"This is Travis with your eight o'clock news. Two men aged 46 and 39 are in custody for the five murders dating back to 1974. More arrests are expected..."

* * *

"This is Travis with your ten o'clock news. Six more men have been arrested in connection with the Splendid Hotel murders and arson of 1974."

* * *

"This is Michelle with your eleven o'clock news. Wilfred Firlotte, 46, and Igor Ivanovich, 39, have been found guilty of conspiracy to commit murder in the death of Nadezhda Logan six years ago..."

* * *

"This is Michelle with your four o'clock news. Walter Messer, 45, Matthew Whipple, 24, Kevin Farley, 32, Jason McClintock, 37,

Marcus Hammond, 38, and Donald Carmichael, 40 have been found guilty of five counts of first degree murder and one count of arson in the 1974 Splendid Hotel tragedy. Vincent Greenfield, Gregory Logan, Nadezhda Logan, Steven Henderson, and Blanche Carleton were murdered and the building was set ablaze. Carleton and Henderson were discovered in the rubble following the tragedy. Greenfield, Logan and Logan were discovered by the riverbank in 1980 during excavations for the Westmorland Street Bridge."

* * *

"This is Michelle with your six o'clock news. Further arrests have been made in connection with the 1974 murders. Two men and a woman are being held."

* * *

"This is Michelle with your ten o'clock news. Bok Heller, 68, and Gwendolyn Giles, 66, have been found guilty of conspiracy to commit arson. Giles has also been found guilty of one count of conspiracy to commit murder. Boris Babayevski, 77, has been found guilty of one count of conspiracy to commit murder. They will be sentenced on November 13th."

Chapter 30/ Daisies From Ashes

They were gathered in Sandi and Peter's living room – Joyce, Olivia, Arlene, Shannon, Sandi and Peter to watch the evening news.

"The children are fast asleep." Sandi said, "They always go to sleep early when they come to stay with Aunt Sandi and Uncle Peter. We must be boring."

The news anchor with the purple tie smiled congenially:

"Nearly eleven years following the grisly murders and the devastating fire which levelled half of Elmdale's business district, there is finally some justice for the families of the murder victims. Eleven people are now serving prison terms. Our correspondent, Joanne Munn is at the site of the former Splendid Hotel...Joanne."

"Rafe, I am at the corner of Queen and Westmorland Streets, where Splendid Hotel once stood proud, with its blue mosaic tile façade and popular family restaurant on the main floor. Splendid Hotel was a modest, affordable building where the tenants were close friends with one another." the unassuming brunette in the tan trench coat was standing where our front door once had been, "Over ten years ago, on March 19th, 1974, Splendid Hotel was the scene of five gruesome murders and a devastating fire, involving two separate murder plots and an arson plot. One of the victims, Nadezhda Logan, was four months pregnant at the time of her death. She was the intended target of both murder plots – one by her own parents and one by a romantic rival. As you can see behind me, Rafe, the citizens of Elmdale are paying their tributes to the victims by placing flowers and teddy bears." she moved aside to provide a more unobstructed view, "Now that all of the perpetrators have finally been brought to justice, hopefully, healing can begin for the survivors. A foundation has been set up by Vincent Greenfield's widow, Joyce, for adult victims of parental abuse. It is named 'Remember Nadya'. Back to you, Rafe."

* * *

Our corner is smaller since they've widened Westmorland Street to accommodate the added traffic for the shiny new bridge. Newman and Carr is no longer in business. There is an event planner and a travel agency in the aging building. It appears lethargic with modern mismatched windows and a black aluminum roof. Eat-Rite is closed and boarded up, awaiting demolition. But, on that small patch of overgrown grass and weeds we once called home, daisies are flourishing with unabashed flamboyance, their roots nourished by the ashes of our memories. Daisies, the harbingers of eternal hope and love, are parading their splendor for the world to see.

The time has come for me to cross over to join my Harold. A smiling Vincent is walking toward me, liberated from his brief reincarnation. He embraces me.

"Thank you for taking care of them, Mrs. C."

"I'm going to miss all of you."

"We'll all be reunited one day, and we'll never have to return to earth again."

"How are Nadya, Greg and Steve, dear?"

"Living new lives with no memory of this one – but it's temporary. All the pieces will come together soon, Mrs. C."

"Will you be here until then, Vincent?"

"I'm not going anywhere." he smiles.

"Have you seen Lena, dear?"

"I spent considerable time with her. She is happy at last. I'll walk you to the pedway." he takes my arm, "Harold's anxious to see you, but he realizes you had an important mission."

"Thank you, dear." I step on to the light-filled glass pedway, "Till we meet again, Vincent."

"Till we all meet again, Mrs. C." he remains there and waves at me until I reach Harold's long-awaited embrace.

* * *

Joyce would tuck her children into bed that night, kiss their tender cheeks, and turn out the light. She would turn in early with a Psychology textbook and fall asleep with her reading glasses on. In the morning, when she opened her front door to bring in her newspaper, she would find the bouquet of daisies Vincent placed on the front steps for her.

About The Author:

Summer Seline Coyle is a literary feminist novelist with a B.A. in Sociology and English Literature, and a certificate in Counselling.

Her personal history of extreme abuse, neglect, and injustice is the driving force behind the empathy, tenderness, and passion in her portrayal of her diverse characters. Through her fiction, she hopes to raise public awareness, and be a healing voice for other survivors.

Also By Summer Coyle:

SCORPIONS HUNT BY NIGHT
SANDCASTLES IN THE RAIN
SUMMER IS A SHORT SEASON
SUMMER'S ECHO (formerly SANCTUARY)

CPSIA information can be obtained
at www.ICGtesting.com
Printed in the USA
LVHW100238270422
717347LV00003B/52

9 781778 133725